The Memoir of

Marilyn Monroe

THE MEMOIR

OF MARILYN MONROE

Edited by Sandi Gelles-Cole

Published by Gelles-Cole Literary Enterprises
P.O. Box 341
Woodstock, NY 12498
www.LiteraryEnterprises.com
www.TheMemoirOfMarilynMonroe.com

Cover design: Juan Carlos Barrientos (COWDesign.com)
Author photo: Kenneth Salzmann

ISBN 0-9786621-3-x

This book is a work of fiction. All people and private institutions, corporate or official entities described in THE MEMOIR OF MARILYN MONROE are either fictitious or used fictitiously.

DEDICATED TO:

Joey, who saved my life
Joe, the dog who saved me
Joe D, everyone's hero
Reggie, for teaching me
the meaning of consequences
And to KAS, for everything else

DRAMA QUEEN
June 1, 2011

They say only the good die young and I guess it's true because I'm still here. Today is my eighty-fifth birthday. During these years I have lived three lives: Before Marilyn, Being Marilyn and After.

I created Marilyn Monroe and then men molded her: studios, agents, and husbands. Ever since the night I did not die, I have tried to leave her behind, but wherever I went, the creature followed. I tried to run. I tried changing my name, my country of residence, my hair color, body type, career and sexual preference. I went to college for coursework in Humanities and studied Russian Literature. But there was no escaping her. The character I created became my own personal monster and devoured me in the '50s, and even after she died I could no more be someone else than I could grow a penis, change my skin color, or stop being a movie star.

My so-called death scene is always described the same: My housekeeper, Eunice Murray, finds my wasted, naked body tangled in a sheet, wet from secretions better left unexplained. I am face down with one hand hanging over the telephone. This detail is discussed often; am I answering a call or making one and if I am calling, then whom?

But it did not happen that way. I cheated death. Eunice Murray administered an enema of chloral hydrate on the orders of my psychiatrist, Ralph Greenson. My psychiatrist wanted me dead because he could no longer contain me. Eunice Murray wanted me dead because I had fired her and this was her last day on the job. But they didn't succeed, and the reported sightings of Marilyn Monroe still walking the earth are absolutely true. Because here's what happened.

On the night of August 4, 1962, young Joey DiMaggio the third--that is the Yankee Clipper's son -- on leave from Camp Pendleton where he served in the Marines -- arrived on the doorstep of Palm Drive, my home in Brentwood at 8PM.

No sound announced his arrival; nothing in my world stirred. He was tall, like his father, but with a fuller face, so his nose was not quite so prominent. Probably the lamp over the doorbell cast a diligent spotlight over his jaw, creating a moody study in light and shadow, the kind of shot you might see in a *noir* film from the '40s.

Joey was kinder than his father. He had a heart bigger than the new Yankee Stadium and he used to fill it with people, not always the nicest kind. DiMaggio the father might have been the last American knight, but it was his son who saved my life.

Joey and I were close from the time he was ten, when Clipper Joe and I were courting the first time. We shared the same disease, which become evident in Joey by the time he was in his early teens.

I can't say he was like a child to me, because that would demean the memory of his mother, Dorothy Olsen DiMaggio. I was a scandal to the DiMaggio family and this book is meant only to tell what really happened and to make amends where I can. So let's say Joey was more like my nephew.

He had broken his engagement and wanted to talk. Joey had a key to every place I ever lived but I imagine before he let himself in that he stood for a few minutes at the doorway where the bougainvillea had lately blossomed in time for my birthday.

Always around my birthday everywhere I make sure there is the sweet scent of hibiscus, bougainvillea, lilies and lilacs.

I was a spring baby.

No one could ever take that away from me.

***

My backyard was a perfumery because prior to my "death," Joe D and I had planned to remarry on August 8, and I had arranged for a profusion of flowers and flowering shrubs to be planted around the garden. There were lilacs, bougainvillea, and hibiscus, of course, and yellow roses. I had overdone it really, but what didn't I overdo? The colors and the fragrance gave me pleasure right up until the moment on that night in August when I lost consciousness and the third part of my life began: After Marilyn.

I suspect Joey debated whether or not to come in. The DiMaggios are a formal group, even today, a classic Italian family and good manners are inbred. But Joey was 20 years old and broken -hearted so he turned to me for comfort while I was dying in the bedroom from an overdose.

I was swimming around in a morbid, horrible darkness. What I remember is his khaki hat as he bent over me and laid his young man's mouth over mine. "What are you doing?" I was struggling to say. It was a bad dream. It had to be, because here was my sweet Joey trying to kiss me, just like all of the men in Hollywood who had bought me then brought me down -- Zanuck, Wilder, Charlie Feldman, ARTHUR MILLER. And now Joey? No, please God, no. It must be that I was going stark raving mad. Just like my mother.

"Marilyn, breathe, please breathe." I felt something inside me stir. I had died a couple of times before from a combination of Seconal, Nembutal, chloral hydrate and alcohol, so I knew about the lungs stopping and the brain not getting enough air.

"Marilyn?"

?" The set had changed, and the actors. Now it was Deadpan Joe DiMaggio, the father, talking to me. I didn't know where I was but there were lots of curtains, lights. In retrospect, of course, I know it as the Cedars Sinai emergency room.

Somehow, yet again, I had managed not to die. The taste of charcoal informed me my stomach had been pumped. I didn't remember attempting suicide so I figured it was probably a good thing that I hadn't died. I was too stupefied to consider whether or not the overdose was accidental or attempted homicide.

Drugs and terror pulled me under the cover of unconsciousness again. My sleep was fitful.

I was aware of movement. I felt something stir, or sensed something, and I tried to respond.

Then my mind and body went dark.

***

Many days dragged by, some of them, thankfully, under the cover of unconsciousness. If you have never detoxed from barbiturates, then I will explain it simply as having your body serve as host to your own personal reptile and spider farm.

Things crawled over me and under me and before my eyes. My nervous system felt like someone was playing screeching atonal tunes on it all night long. My ears rang and over the ringing there were voices.

This was before the Beatles, the mass marketing of LSD, and peyote trips, so I had no frame of reference for what I was going through. I only knew that crazy people saw things; my mother heard voices and had been in a locked-down ward on and off much of the time that I could remember.

I could no longer imagine going on one more day with my life as I had been living it.

I was finished.

I did not know what that meant. I only knew I was lying on the floor of a room that seemed more like a bedroom than a hospital.

***

There was one woman who was there whenever I awoke, but she didn't even wear a uniform. Occasionally she administered a drug I suppose was Librium. The only difference between day and night was that varying patterns of light would shift across my face, or not. Whatever kind of woman I had been before, I was not her now. I was not even human anymore. There was no chance that I could eat or shower or dress myself. I could crawl to the toilet near the bed, puke, then collapse back onto the floor. Once in a while the woman or another woman pretty much like her would put me back in the bed, and the next time I needed to crawl towards the toilet I just stayed on the floor.

After a few days, the dragging-myself-to-the-toilet-and-puking phase came to an end. If I had considered myself an insomniac before, now I was a vampire, trolling the halls at night. This was when I realized I was not in a hospital but in a house I did not recognize. There seemed to be no one in any of the other rooms.

The kitchen gave no clues about other residents or my location. I foraged through all the cabinets looking for booze, of course.

But that was pointless, for whoever had harbored drunks here knew to remove not only the liquor but any product whatsoever that might contain alcohol, including cooking extracts and cleaners.

I asked the woman watcher for mouth wash but she just shook her head. Not in a judgmental way, just like she knew there was a yearning.

Medicine cabinets in two separate bathrooms yielded: Band-Aids, aspirin, Pepto Bismol, Alka Seltzer. I would have killed the woman watching me if she stood between me and a shot of ethyl alcohol, but there was none. Definitely this house had been alcoholic-proofed. Hand sanitizers were only for medical people back then but if there had been any it would have been down the hatch. Not a second's thought.

My mind was not clear. If you've never been seriously poisoned by drugs and alcohol let me explain: a penetrating fog has taken over your brain. Imagine Ireland or England, the moors. I shot The Prince and The Showgirl with Olivier in England and the weather was suicide-friendly. The fog would crawl in your mouth when you slept and cover your chest and keep you from waking up so it would take pills with your coffee to wake you.

But here there were no pills.

I couldn't remember the way back to the room I was staying in lots of times. But it was worse than that. I couldn't remember my last thought. I had always had trouble remembering my lines. It was a source of great embarrassment. Co-stars assumed I was acting like a prima donna but that is not true.

Most of the time I was in my dressing room crying because there would be empty spaces in my head where my lines had been just that morning.

Not only were the drugs rotting holes through the solid places, but all the stuff of my past and the selling of my self to get where I wanted to go were eating away at my mind, too, and I was losing pieces of my brain. This is where the lines leaked out.

While detoxing I could feel words and thoughts being soaked up into the vapors of poison that had taken over inside my head. As I remember it, my body was screaming out for more poison and my mind was on strike. Something had shut down up there and refused to operate until it got more poison. My head had broken open and everything inside had emptied out. I absolutely despised Joey DiMaggio for saving me.

I was out of hope. I did not want to die but I wasn't all that anxious to go on living, if you could call this living. I was tired of drugs and men and being in the public eye.

In fact, I was flat out exhausted.

If I never did anything or saw anyone for the rest of my life, that would be fine. I especially didn't want to see or hear from anyone I knew, and at the top of that list were my agent, my lawyer, and the studio.

I came up with an image of myself as a tree in a rain forest, my blonde head the top, all shiny in the sun, and my feet the roots buried deep in the mud which was churning with bugs and icky things, but fecund. Something inside me was saying to stay planted and let the forest do the work. The idea to disappear was budding.

This was what I was pondering when two women showed up. One of the women was tall and butch looking, in her forties. It's ironic that I thought that because I learned later that her last name was Mann. She knocked on the bedroom door, and without waiting for me to invite her, she came in. Just sort of assumed, if you know what I mean.

She basically pulled another woman along with her. The other woman was younger, smaller. She was intimidated by me, so I smiled at her automatically, turning on my Marilyn face to put her at ease.

"I'm Marguerite, this is Sue," said the older one.

"I'm Marilyn."

At this the younger one kind of broke up laughing and we all got the joke. I mean, I was not wearing any make-up at all, just Wranglers and a sweater, but to Sue, I think I seemed still a movie star. I asked if they needed money for a donation or something.

"No," Marguerite said. Her eyes were dark, fathomless and profound. Wounded. "I've flown all the way from New York to see if we can help you stop killing yourself with drugs."

"But how did you know."

"Don't worry about that."

Marguerite told me all about being a socialite and drinking her way down the scale until she had nowhere to turn, and how this program she would tell me about had saved her and could save me, too.

. It could help me stop the endless cycle of booze and drugs, help me stop putting myself to sleep with Nembie enemas and waking myself up with the hypodermic needles I now filled with my own personalized drug cocktail.

Then Sue talked while Marguerite kept her probing eyes on me. I was comfortable around lesbians and this did not seem like a lustful stare.

"But I can't exactly be anonymous."

"Just come with us," Marguerite said. "You'll be surprised who's there."

Something made me tell her the truth without editing myself. "I'm afraid of being spotted. I'm thinking of never showing up out there again." I looked from one to the other. "You know, disappearing. I... I don't want people to know that I'm alive."

"That can happen," Marguerite said gently. "We can help you with that. It's safe where we are taking you."

I heard *safe* and my whole being relaxed. The woman watcher seemed totally OK about me leaving with Marguerite and Sue.

I allowed myself to be taken to a small town outside of Hollywood where we went downstairs to the basement of a church and I sat in the back of a smoky room and listened. That night I understood that I had been taken from the hospital by a person in a room like this who had given over their home to me for shelter. A sober house it would be called now. A safe house. A place to recover for a while

Every day or night, sometimes both, I was taken to a room like this one where I was gentled back to sanity. I would say now that I was carried rather than taken. In a while it was time to move on and make room for whichever drunk was behind me needing safety.

I decided I was ready to live by myself and rented an efficiency apartment by the week right near the West Hollywood house where most of the meetings were held, which eventually became what is known as a clubhouse.

I did take Maf the poodle with me. Joey had taken him onto the base for the weeks I was gone, because his father would have nothing to do with a gift I received from Frank Sinatra.

So, the poodle had finally gotten housebroken by the Marine Corps.

Joe was notified and came to help me move. Marguerite Mann impressed on him the importance of my staying close to Sue and the other people I had met. She talked rings around Joe. It would have been funny except I had lost my sense of humor. I tried to reach down into myself to find some sense of who I was but I was a hollow bucket. I felt like if anybody dropped a stone down my throat it would rattle around and make a lot of noise. Life was taking place far away from me, so this bit about who was taking me and where did not matter too much. It registered that Joe was angry, but I did not care.

***

I listened every day for a long time, sitting in the back of the rooms. At first I couldn't think, sleep, eat or walk. Joe kept asking when we were going to reschedule the wedding and he started doing that pushy thing again, wondering when I was going to stop "sneaking" off to these out-of-the-way meetings

I was now tied to the DiMaggios with a secret and Joe didn't let me forget it for a moment. In turn, I withheld affection from him. The thought of him touching me made me want to go numb, and that would make me start to think about where I might get my hands on some barbiturates.

I was living in an etherized world, not questioning anything. Writers I read knew just how to describe my feelings. Chekhov knew. Dostoevsky knew. Miller could not have described the world I was living in because it was a world that was being drawn by feelings and spirit.

My head was nowhere in it.

Eventually I took another step toward the living. It had been six weeks since my so-called suicide, and I realized that if I were dead my money would be dispersed.

I had left most of my worldly possessions to Lee Strasberg with explicit instructions to keep a percentage of the liquid assets as well as royalties that would come due for The Actors Studio.

There was also a list of the people to whom I wanted him to disperse a portion of the liquid assets, as well as personal possessions and an amount set up for Mother's long term care.

Obviously I needed to keep a portion of the estate for my future. I spoke to Sue nightly. We came up with a plan.

***

In the club for drunks my story was that I was a Marilyn Monroe impersonator. Without makeup, my hair growing out chestnut blonde, never styled, and my daily uniform of jeans and large tee shirts, I could get away with it. Or maybe people were on to me and I did not know it. Whatever the truth was, in those days Anonymous meant something. It wasn't like now when every celebrity who behaves badly joins the club to erase the stain on his reputation. People's businesses and families were at risk if they were known alcoholics and we kept each other's secrets.

I asked Joey to retrieve the original copy of my will from the house on Palm Drive. Naturally there was a lawyer in the meetings -- he had been a raving drunk --and he reworked the will for me.

One of the women was a notary public. One thing people have to know is that this tribe of mine can always band together and, as a unit, come up with solutions. Drunks are smart, and they have usually spent some time living double lives. That makes them incredibly resourceful.

If we find our way back from the precipice, we tend to prevail.

If we don't, we die horrible, slow and ugly deaths, usually in jails or psychiatric hospitals.

Now I could regain many of the liquid assets previously left to the Actor's Studio. I wanted to keep the rights to my promotion images such as the famous photo from *The Seven Year Itch*, but I had to figure out how the money would be filtered to me. I formed an open trust managed by Joe. To make certain everything went according to plan, I left some jewelry to Sue so she would be in attendance at the probate meeting. The revised will was "discovered" by the DiMaggios as they were going through my personal possessions. Greene, my former partner and lawyer, to his credit was still grieving when he contacted Sue to come for the reading of the will. I drove down to Hollywood to loan her my best black suit. Part of me enjoyed the game. It would take a while, but there would be enough money to live on. Strasberg still had a huge share plus the percentage to disburse. The balance was left for Gladys.

So I was living in the West Hollywood efficiency. As each day went by, my senses were reborn. Nothing ever tasted more important than my morning cup of coffee. I woke each day and scrambled to the tiny 1930s style kitchenette to percolate a cup of the Brazilian coffee I was drinking in those days, very chichi. After one cup of coffee and a sweet roll I would put on some Capri pants and a sweater, careful to wear a bra as Marilyn never did.

I had lost a great deal of weight from laying off the booze. My curves were not so outsized. I wore the large sunglasses Mrs. Kennedy was making stylish. Someone would have to get really close to recognize me. Outside, I greeted the sun with my naked face, the burden lifted of having to report to "Make-Up and Hair". I started to understand that a person could be happy for herself, that you did not need an audience to smile. It was an awakening.

There was a routine to my day. No one had ever taught me the significance of a beginning, middle and end. I knew about story structure, acts, character arcs, but never had this had any bearing on life. Suddenly I understood that my life, my days and hours, had arcs and rhythms and that there was a reason families had dinner hours, and if I had a dinner hour it might translate to my having a family. Everything was new. I was learning how to be a human being rather than a star. I was learning to be a person who could be part of a family rather than a star who might survive only as part of a constellation.

Joe visited from San Francisco. At the end of August he arrived bearing gifts. There was the usual bottle of Chanel Number 5. The scent was no longer working for me. Maybe detox had changed the chemistry of my skin, but the perfume turned acidic and I had already hidden the bottle he had brought me when I left the sober house.

The box from Harry Winston was more ominous, a black velvet ring box. Joe wasn't a big spender, as anyone can tell you. His big night out was dinner at Toots Shor's. He let the box sit on the table between us without saying anything.

I'm sure there was a game on the television of one kind or another. Out of the corner of my eye I saw him glance my way and the yawning pit in my stomach stretched under my ribcage.

I wanted a drink. I excused myself.

"Where are you going?"

"I'm going to the powder room."

"No you're not, you're going to call that dyke, Sue."

He was right. I needed to talk to Sue because it was her I spoke to if I felt a yearning for a drink and a pill.

But Joe had another idea.

Before I could exit, he had his arm around my waist and was pulling me back. This was no romantic scene he was playing out. He grabbed my hand and pulled me down to the chair next to the table where the black velvet box sat, a threat.

The bungalow had windows open to the street and I saw a man walking his dog oblivious to my predicament. My house on Palm Drive was closed off to the street with blackout curtains, a familiar décor for those addicted to drugs.

In those Hollywood Marilyn Monroe years, people attributed this idiosyncrasy to my insomnia. I realize now that those curtains made my home what it was -- an early version of a crack house. I had kept Marilyn locked up and now she was facing a man driven to distraction by a lesbian.

Joe went berserk. The ring from Harry Winston stayed neat in its velvet black box on top of a cheap wooden table, but the box fell when Joe knocked me down with one huge sock to my jaw. Slugger Joe.

He left without his hat or his Harry Winston jewelry box. There would be no police report. I had suffered his black eyes before. Here was the miracle. I called Marguerite Mann, I called Sue, I went to sleep. The next morning I put on sunglasses and went to one of those church basements. There was no need for pills or alcohol.

ST. ALBANS MEMORIAL HOSPITAL
Portland, Oregon, 2011

The nurse who takes care of me in this hospital is Cherie, an odd coincidence, as will become clear. Each of the ten days I have been here my wounds are checked and cleaned. Cherie is the only nurse allowed to see beneath the bandages.

Cherie is Romanian; as she works, she will tell stories of her time as a sex slave and how she escaped from a trafficker who had purchased her when she was twelve. The stories stab me with her pain but they also put my own trouble in perspective.

"Good morning, Cherie." I try to smile but my bandages won't let me. "You have the big tub."

"It is Wednesday," she replies.

I remember that last week, on Wednesday, I guess, she had immersed me in a sort of portable spa with a salty taste. The bath is pointless, really, just a way to have someone lay their hands on me, offering the healing touch, human contact. After that, Cherie walks me into the French shower, me naked and Cherie in an ugly one-piece bathing suit. She holds me up while the seven shower heads beat against my ridiculous old sunken shell. Sometimes she sings very softly.

. I am certain she was a very able prostitute because she expresses complete neutrality about my nakedness. Her touch is tender but efficient. She is smaller than I am, but her arms hold me up securely. Her long thick braid is all the way down her back to her waist. Once I've had enough of the water therapy she will take me back to bed or perhaps we will walk in the garden outside.

My body submerged beneath the bath water is foreign to me. I am wrinkled, my outsized breasts droop. My coloring is very fair and my pubic area is hairless like any other old woman. I am less gorgeous than Georgia O'Keefe. I still think of sex and finally it is with a soft lens, dreamy, pretty.

Sex is over there and I don't need to yank it or work to make it rise. Sensuality is wherever it wants to be without endeavor. Very old men still find me attractive – or they did until recently. I think that is the natural order of the world and it makes me believe in God.

Cherie tells me about the others who live in this part of the hospital where much reconstructive surgery is done. Many are wounded soldiers. Some, she tells me, ache and suffer from loneliness. It astonishes me that I am not one of those lonely hearts.

Me, Marilyn Monroe, who squeezed the last drop of affection out of everyone around until they had to go.

Now I am alone, but not afraid. Only indecisive.

I lived long enough so that finally faith fulfilled me. The decision whether to go ahead at my age with a serious operations is really only a small one.

In a one-act play the audience would be thinking, so live or die already, we need to go to the bathroom. We need a cocktail.

But who will play me in the movie?

***

I left Los Angeles after the incident with Joe.

For the first time in my entire life no one was telling me what to do and all of these other people in the church basements were showering me with good attention, listening, backing off if I needed them to, but talking to me if that is what I wanted.

For someone who was surer of her identity this would have been great but for me it was actually dangerous.

If I was not Marilyn Monroe anymore, and Norma Jean was undesirable, I was lost to myself.

***

There weren't a lot of women in the healing rooms back then, and there were a fair number of craggy characters, little more than bums. At this point I looked more like Norma Jean would have looked at 36 than anything like Marilyn. I started wearing a baseball hat so the brim would shield my face. I sat in the back of smoky rooms with a cup of coffee and listened while everybody smoked and talked about staying sober.

There was a guy of course, because in my mid-thirties, there would have to be a man. I was never without a man.

I only went without a man at a point during my sixties and that was a fluke. My life is the story of searching for my perfect stranger. I'm still searching.

I found my knight but he died and now I'm writing this memoir at 85 years old and I'm still waiting for the perfect Prince Charming to walk through the door.

At my age I'm not sure if that is hopeful or depressing.

The anonymity of the program was beginning to tantalize me, probably not in a good way. I was no longer hiding from the world in order to protect my health and healing.

I was running from everyone, especially the people who really knew me.

Pat Lawford had been my best friend. I was due at a dinner party at her home the night I did not die.

Pat had decreed me an honorary Kennedy which was not said lightly; Frank Sinatra was my trusted ally. We had been platonic roommates for a brief time. People assumed we were lovers at that time, but we were not. He was still mourning Ava Gardner.

These and a few others would have kept my secret until I wanted to go public again and if that had been the case what a different story this would have been. But Marilyn's entire life was precarious.

It was a dangerous history. It was from MM I needed to run. I had rented a cabin in a little town way up North like a character from central casting looking for trouble in a movie directed by John Huston. There I met the next man I thought might save me. Wednesday nights there was a candlelight meeting in a Methodist Church, with the soft, forgiving glow of five or so candles the only illumination in the room. I had started wearing makeup again and my hair was cut short and geometric. Not platinum anymore, but not chestnut brown either. Maybe honey blonde. I was still real thin, less than my usual 117 pounds, and out of context, people forgot all about Marilyn Monroe. The world did not talk about her for a while after I died, if you recall. If she had not really died, then she was a hopeless drunk, off somewhere in a lunatic asylum.

Basically I was out of the news.

Finally, at one meeting, I raised my hand and said, "My name is Cherie and I am an alcoholic." That was crazy, of course. But Cherie, the chanteuse in *Bus Stop* had somehow popped out and claimed me.

It was eerie.

I remembered how Greenson, my psychiatrist, had started spreading the word around town that I was schizophrenic.

Perhaps he was right. Maybe all those performances had only worked because I had turned into Lorelei and Rose Loomis and Sugar Kane Kowalczyk.

But no, I wouldn't buy that. What was happening was that I was tired of everyone wanting to own a piece of me. Everyone wanting a piece, but nobody loving me or knowing me. This was a chance for me to start over. So that night I began to create Cherie.

During the cake break, I sat down for coffee with the two other women in the group I had already met.

Rules were very strict; men stayed with the men and women with the women. But I could see that one of the younger men, maybe forty, was looking at me out of the corner of his eye, while he was pretending to be listening to the group he was standing with.

When the meeting reconvened, we all went back for another half hour , then broke up with The Lord's Prayer and said our goodnights. At the door to the church basement this gentleman asked if he could accompany me to my automobile.

"Sure," I said, and I can still recall that it did not sound the least bit like me at all. No whispery Marilyn. In fact, to this day I have never heard that wispy siren's voice again.

The man was tall and lanky. I had not seen such an innocent in real life since leaving Bakersfield. Later I realized he was not unlike the Don Murray character in Bus Stop, the way he looked anyway.

In the moment at the car I thought of cloying sweet sodas, egg creams, kissing with closed mouths-- going way back to the beginning.

How ridiculous, since we were both at a meeting of recovering drunks and therefore each had a past. But none of that mattered. He smelled delicious, something like pine and amber. And he wore khaki work pants and a blue short sleeve tee shirt with another shirt over it. Men did not dress like that, not businessmen nor recovering alcoholics who tended to wear suits they had just bought with their first few dollars from the Salvation Army. He could be anyone or anything I wanted him to be so long as I did not ask any questions.

I was not born beautiful. Furthermore, I was raised as a serial obsession. When Gladys failed to succeed in using me to obtain her dreams, she unloaded me. Then there were the faux protectors: The Bolanders, The McKees, Doc Goddard, that pervert, Jimmy Dougherty. (Jimmy was nice enough, I can't really blame him.) Then along came Hollywood: Ben Lyon, Johnny Hyde, Howard Cohn, John Huston. They all shared the compulsion to remake me. I had no idea how the world worked outside of movies. Like a chameleon I had no color until you placed me in a situation. And I only knew how to speak like they talk in the movies. So I drew on Cherie.

"You're Cherie? I'm..."

I stuck out my hand to shake his before he spoke his name, an odd way to misdirect the dialogue, but the only way I had. It befuddled him enough to accomplish the purpose.

"Good to meet you. My car is right over there. "I was wearing a knee-length dotted Swiss cotton sundress, and my words were twanging like I had just stepped off a bus from Arkansas.

I led him to the navy blue 1954 Olds for which I had traded in my Cadillac. I used the extra cash – which I kept in the cabin rather than in a bank -- to live on so that I would not need to contact Joe and he would not be able to trace me. Even when I started out this foray I was thinking like a sneak; I should have realized at the time that I was heading for trouble.

"Alright then, so…" He opened the door and I slid behind the wheel.

"See you next week." I smiled. I wondered if he could see me in the darkness and if so what was my expression projecting?

After a few weeks of seeing "him" once a week at meetings I allowed the man to introduce himself as Ed Digby, a car salesman. That almost killed the romance right there, but I was willing to pick and choose what I wanted to hear.

Mr. Digby was a gentleman, and we were never alone in any event, always with other people, going out for coffee after meetings. During the walks we took while the others ate I wove a complex tale comprised of all the roles I had played.

I was Cherie Mortenson, a sixth grade school teacher who was leaving a terrible marriage to an abusive drunk not willing to put the drink down.

Obviously I could cry and laugh on cue. I was terrible to this man, trapping him in a tapestry of Byzantine lies and sucking the juice out of him. He didn't have a chance. No matter that I told him I'd be leaving and he shouldn't fall hard for me. At the same time I'd be coaxing him on with my Cherie smile and my cocked little finger, *Come closer*. He was helplessly entranced. What did I expect would happen?

Things got out of control. He went plum crazy when I actually did get ready to leave town.

Digby went out drinking and ended up at my cabin drunk. He tried to force himself on me, begging me not to go and telling me all of his sloppy feelings.

That was when I dropped the little girl innocence and got tough. I changed character as quick as you can say Rose Loomis, and he snapped to and realized I was not anything that I said I was. I think I saw his heart shatter on the floor and scatter into the corners of my cabin.

I called his friend, Sean, who came and got him. Ed was crying and banging his head against the wall and Sean took him off to the hospital. Before the night was over, though, Sean came back to tell me just what he thought of me.

"Wait a minute, I didn't pour that booze down Mr. Digby's throat," I said. By this point I had called Sue to tell my side of things and I was feeling fairly self-righteous.

"You're trouble, Cherie."

Sue was on the phone and my hand over the receiver didn't cover up Sean's voice. "Cherie? Who's Cherie"?

"I'll call you back," I said.

Sometimes you really do have to run no matter what anybody says. The next day I was on the road and didn't look back.

CUBA
October, 1962

I crawled back to Southern California, but through the back door.

I drove down the Pacific Coast Highway to Joey's bachelor pad. I knew he always hid a key. After sneaking around to make sure no one was home, I decided I could stay there one night while I decided my next move.

Joey's apartment had clearly not been cleaned in a while and it was too disgusting to bathe or sleep there, so I found the few cleaning products he had and went after the place.

Truth be told I knew nothing about house cleaning -- why would I?

But I put on an old Yankees cap to keep my hair clean and an old Yankees sweatshirt of Joey's that went down to my knees and I got to work. Catching a look of myself in the bathroom mirror I thought I looked like a prepubescent young woman dressed for Halloween.

By evening I was exhausted in that way where your muscles ache but your mind is free. Like you're ready to read *People* magazine, though in those days I was reading *Women's Day* and *Family Circle.* I read those women's shelter magazines like they were lucky charms that could bring me a real husband and a baby.

So I had them in my suitcase and was reading one when the key turned in the lock.

I didn't have time to worry. Joey would never blow my cover. For one thing, he knew all about his father's abusive temper. For another, Joey loved me more than he loved his father. If he had to pick sides, I was certain he would pick mine.

The door opened on a petite woman with thick, black shiny hair piled up on her head and eyes the color of black grapes. I spoke no Spanish but figured out she was the cleaning lady.

We agreed, using sign language and her broken English, that the apartment had been a hazard area and that I had straightened up. She informed me she was engaged only once a month. I gave her four hundred dollars and told her to start coming every week and I would make sure she got more money.

It was only afterward that I realized how lucky I was to have on those ridiculous cleaning clothes.

But the incident brought me to the next level of understanding my predicament. The rest of my life was becoming a possibility. I needed to plan for it,

Any half-baked thought I might have had about returning to the world had been trampled by the fact that around this time the whole world, it seemed, had one day just upped and decided that the Marilyn Monroe mode was out of style.

The Housewives' Syndrome was crying out for exploration.

The female ideal had slimmed down two sizes since the War. Metaphorically speaking, I would be better off dead to a certain kind of woman.

I think some people believed I killed myself because there was no future for a forty year old curvy sex bomb. We girls were taking ourselves far too seriously by that time.

God knows my family such as it was would not be happy if I reappeared. My mother, I heard, did not react when told Marilyn had died that day in August. My half-sister, Berniece could not afford to come to California to claim the "body."

I had made a neat escape all things considered, and gotten away from the burden of the creature who had finally hit rock bottom. There was no longer a place for a character whose role was to help Americans discover that sex could be fun and funny. There was an easy to use birth control pill on the market.

The revolutions were coming.

Which is why I turned again to DiMaggio. It was wrong, but I did it all the same.

Joe believed in the half-assed conspiracy theory that the Kennedys wanted me assassinated and I fed this paranoia, convincing him that I needed to go underground. And on my own behalf I have to say it's not like he was a total innocent.

He wanted me all to himself and he thought he could keep me if the world thought I had died.

I let Joe play the hero once again, like he always wanted to do. He met me at the airport and we went to that horrible place he kept in Florida.

We agreed that I should leave the country for a while. Cuba seemed a good starting place but getting there was a problem. Prime Minister Castro had recently declared his allegiance to the Soviets and put a stop to all transportation from the States to Havana.

The sad part of this was the end of the railway connection, especially the Havana Special, a daily luxury train from New York City to a boat line out of Miami and on to Havana.

So we needed another way.

A lot of people don't know that for a time after his baseball career and before he was the face for Mr. Coffee, Joe worked as a post-war military supplier. What that means I'm not sure, but it gave him access to military bases and career soldiers.

Anyway, Joe epitomized the best of America and many doors were open to him.

Under his role as a military supplier, he managed to get me a place on a run to Guantanamo.

He had no trouble grabbing one of the few seats on the small plane for me. I was met at the airport by a small caravan of camouflage jeeps and escorted to Havana, where a turquoise blue adobe house had been found for me to rent.

There was no worrying that information about me was going anywhere

. Cuba might as well have been land locked. Certainly it was locked down. I still think of this whenever Guantanamo Bay is mentioned. How locked up it was, and isolated. Far away.

I have to say Castro treated me like royalty. When he called me Cherie, his accent surrounding the 'ch' sounded like a caress. My hair framed a face made thinner along with my troubles. No more red lips or bedroom blue eyes. I was no longer kittenish. In fact, I had turned into a dog rather than a cat. A nice handsome dog, but still no longer feline. If it had been sex Castro had been after, he would have been disappointed. Sex comes and goes for me and this was definitely a no go time.

Havana still had a fresh face back then. I've been there since and the whole country is just a poor wretch, a broken down old lady living on the street in a 1955 Chevy. But back then the part of town I occupied had one foot in Cuba's glorious halcyon days and a leather boot in the communist future, worn in and waiting for orders. There were commandeered mansions and abandoned luscious casinos with rooftop swimming pools.

I was drunk on Cuba from the moment I got there, on the exotic women with erotic looks. Even the poor shop girls knew how to dress, and walked this sultry way. And the men, full of themselves and victory, were burnished peacocks, especially the young ones in uniform.

I might not know how to remember lines, but Spanish came easy to me and within a few months I was talking to my live-in maid and to the driver that had been arranged for me.

Anyway, I loved Cuba. I loved the women, and I loved the young men. I don't mean as sexual objects, but more as objects of art. In short, I was serene in Cuba.

One bright October day, I woke with a great happy feeling. I had been sober for three months, away from the suffocation of Hollywood. Cut adrift, in fact, from the demands of my entire world.

Even my mother's madness was being handled by someone else. Her bills were paid by a trust and that was that.

No one could get to me. Only Sue knew where to reach me. And Marguerite Mann. I had been freed from the mental obsession to drink or use drugs. God had spared me for something, though I am still not sure what.

Only those very close to Fiddle, my nickname for Castro, even knew there was an American woman living under his protection in the country. These were the original radicals from Havana University, the group attached to Che Guevara, true revolutionaries.

These men had been fighting to get rid of Batista and his cronies since 1953 and now, in charge, they still thought of themselves as Rebels of the Sierra Leone and acted like characters in a Sam Spiegel movie.

And I sympathized

. I dressed in clothes that resonated with the revolution -- fatigues, combat boots -- cleaving to this new world I inhabited. Later, when Henry Fonda's baby daughter, Jane, dressed down and went to Hanoi, I thought about my Cuba days. No, Jane Fonda was not the first movie actress to embrace combat fatigues. I suppose I was ahead of my time.

This day, there was a knock on the door. The revolutionary who came to fetch me was Jorges. He was young and bright-eyed, like all of the young men who surrounded Fidel Castro. Jorges said little, which was not his way. He had been essential in helping me learn Spanish. But Jorges was not smiling. His black eyes had a film across them, a distraction.

"What is it?" I might have said. But I said nothing and neither did he. He kept his body apart from mine, which was odd. Usually we fell in step quite naturally, and I noted that we were out of synch, awkward with each other. A voice in my head yelled 'Need a drink' but it passed without my focusing on it.

Thank God for Sue.

She had taught me what to do to shout down those voices. If you do not have the disease of alcoholism, the need for some liquid courage does not sound like a big deal; you take a little snort or you don't. But for us the need is like a homicidal sadist sneaking through the back door. An alcoholic who does not stop drinking will definitely die an alcohol-related death

. The sick evil twin inside each recovered drunk is wanting to die and takes over the brain. Suicide by cop. Suicide by Alcohol, same thing. But Sue was always one slim dime away. I could call her from wherever I was and bill it to my own telephone line.

Sometimes we talked for hours, and sometimes we just said hi, but knowing that there was someone in the world who understood what it was like to want to obliterate my senses, and who knew where I was and what was happening to me – that provided an essential pocket of peace somewhere in my psyche.

Sue held my hand long distance. I knew that later on I would find my way to one of the phones still operating on the island.

But that did not happen that day. Or the next. I did not yet know of the *ménage a trois* playing out between the Castro brothers, Khrushchev, and the Kennedy boys. I would bet my life that it did not end until Bobby was killed. I was witnessing the opening gambit in their nuclear playbook.

I entered the former private home that now housed the government, and I smelled stress and anxiety. It made me think of Gable's body odor just before his heart attack, that metallic scent that goes along with the tang in the mouth I associate with the electric twitch in my brain that precedes depression. It's a cycle. Maybe that's where the expression, 'Things didn't smell right' comes from.

Raul Castro was there and since Raul was in charge of military matters, we had barely met. He is a gentle man compared to his brother, but that day the expression on his face was ferocious and fearful.

Fidel was quiet; the worst of his terrible temper tantrums started that way.

Fidel asked me about John Kennedy's use of speed. I had lived through the Bay of Pigs and I tried to dredge up the history of that debacle, but I was not and still am not as quick on my feet when it comes to facts. I can make things up but I don't do that anymore because that is lying. I knew only that Fidel was asking me what I knew about Kennedy's state of mind and if it was possible that he was taking amphetamines. "Because he sounded nervous, loco, maybe he is changing moods?"

Of course I knew that Jack was constantly taking amphetamines and so did everybody else. But I was no Communist Revolutionary, I was Norma Jean, an American, born and bred, and there was no goddamned way I was going to betray my country or my President, never mind that the fucker had dumped me.

That was the man, not The President.

"Of course not. What are you talking about? He's the President of the United States. Do you run this country drunk on Cuban Rum?"

I was the indignant Roslyn watching them take down Mustangs, and at that very moment I was struck with a yearning to go back home to the world I knew.

Oh God, the need to get back to acting and slip into somebody else overtook me and I wanted to fly out of the room high above Cuba, so high that I could watch it shrinking beneath me, a tiny island next to my huge courageous home.

I wanted to be launched out of here, out of this skin and persona and character and into another mind and soul entirely, so that I was not Norma Jean or Marilyn Monroe or a woman in fatigues or a slinky dress with big boobs or anyone recognizable to anyone, but a whole new woman entirely who no one had ever seen before.

Maybe not even a woman this time. Perhaps I could play a man, or a creature from another planet.

In that very moment, Fidel Castro had thrust me into a separate dimension. I was now struck with an obsession.

I was going somewhere, pushing the new baby out.

This was my future. I was going back to the States. Now, or as soon as they would let me out of here.

"Dr. Field?"

"What?"

I had tuned in as Fidel was asking me something about the president's doctor.

"You know this doctor who gives him the amphetamines?"

Castro was miming an injection in his arm.

I was standing. All the other people in the room were men and they were seated. It was then that I became aware of the fact that I was in danger.

This thought did not dawn on me slowly. One moment I was among the host and his colleagues who had been sheltering me, and the next I was alone in hostile territory.

"I don't know what you're talking about. What is this about?" I looked from Jorges to Fidel. His eyes were crazed. I had seen that look before. He could get crazy if dinner was late, so that did not mean much.

Raul was another matter. He had the reputation of being a stabilizing influence but at that moment he was raving. I can't call it anything else. Pounding on the desk and shouting rapid, brute Spanish I couldn't follow.

It came as a surprise to me when Jorges and another young soldier grabbed me, one on each side, and more or less dragged me out of the room. I hadn't followed much of the Spanish, and I had no clue as to why Fidel and Raul were so furious. *I* hadn't done anything wrong.

When we were almost at the door, Fidel spoke to my back, in English.

"You will tell us everything you know about Mr. Kennedy. Or you will starve to death in Cuba."

I started to giggle. It was, of course, the worst thing I could do, but how could I take him seriously?

All my resources as an actress had prepared me for this, probably my greatest role to date. I was tired of the dumb blonde comedienne roles and *Prisoner of The Revolution* was exactly the role I was looking for. I did not know the world was facing the threat of nuclear war. I just read my lines and followed the blocking.

***

I have only a vague memory of my last day in Havana. It was hot, of course. I had not seen Jorges since two female jailers had locked me in a primitive cell. I was not sure where I was, only that we were not in a good part of town and I was definitely in a jail. The cell was along a wall of cells facing a cement courtyard and I was the only female prisoner there. I think the State did not take prisoners in those early days primarily because they didn't have the money to feed anyone.

Castro was not kidding when he said he would not feed me, but it wasn't a punishment. There were just no meals served. My guard, however, a lovely woman from the outskirts of the city, always shared her afternoon meal with me. I don't know if she had not been told about my sentence or if she just disobeyed.

Later I wondered if she might have gotten in trouble for helping me, but at the time I was so hungry that it never occurred to me to worry about that.

How important was I to Fidel Castro? You might think he would want to keep me as a trophy or hostage. But Fidel does not operate that way. He is a bullshit artist par excellence; he fumes, he makes a lot of noise; he talks too much. But he is not a man to take a woman hostage to show off to another man. I never saw him after the confrontation, but I could get into his head and I knew when Jorges came to escort me to the waiting small plane that Castro was depressed. I could empathize.

So, I was unceremoniously dumped in the Hollywood, Florida airport, which believe me was no prize even back then. I'd be damned if I'd go back to Joe one more time. If I did, even just for the night, he was going to expect favors.

I got drunk instead.

It wasn't pretty, though I don't remember much. I woke up with a strange man -- Cuban, in fact.

The first memory I have is opening my eyes to streaming light behind a moldy and graying gauze curtain. The curtain was draped across a gasping air conditioner and it must have been the machine that woke me, for it was as loud as the engine of an automobile enclosed in a garage.

Tentatively I moved my leg, which was unclothed, and felt a hairy leg beside me. Who could it be but a stranger? I jumped, carrying the blanket along with me for cover.

A tawny man, probably in his early thirties, awoke

I will always remember his eyes, jade green, smiling, friendly. I flipped through the characters in my repertoire but there was none to handle this part and I had only Norma Jean. But wait, I had my mother.

Many men had passed through the apartment in Van Nuys and often I was there, or I would see Mother soon after. I slipped into the mind of a deranged woman. I was still partly drunk so it wasn't hard.

First I slapped him. I learned that from my mother, who used to slap men after she slept with them so she would get either a proposal (it never happened) or money. I threatened to call the police. The man spoke very little English but sputtered out that I had picked him up, not the other way around.

I did not want the details. Pointing my finger, I commanded him to leave.

Then I had to face my conscience. Really, when you came down to it, I could get away with drinking and not telling anyone. I would just sober up and go on about my business. Who would know? I tried this idea on, but there was no way I could do it. I could pretend to be a lot of things, but I could not lie about my sobriety.

I called Sue and told her I had slipped. Sue was very quiet, listening.

"I don't remember anything ,just that I woke up in a hotel with a stranger. I don't know where I am except that it is Florida. I left Cuba yesterday."

Sue warned me that it was not going to be so easy to get back on track again. "Nonsense," I declared.

I stayed drunk for two years.

***

I could not get out of Florida. I formed my own turgid lost triangle though mine was more of a slash; from Miami, to the Keys, from the Keys to Tampa.

My plan was to clean up and get sober in Miami. I needed costumes. I had left all my clothes in Cuba and hoped that Sariah, my maid there, had helped herself to the jeans, tee shirts and sundresses. Hollywood, Florida was not the place to shop for clothes

The I-95 was complete in many places or it met up with the Sunshine State or Dixie Highway so driving there was not difficult, but I did not trust myself behind the wheel so I hired a car and driver.

I checked into the Fontainebleau, dismissed the driver, and went straight to their salon where I returned my hair to platinum blonde.

Miami shopping was upscale and cabs were plentiful. I bought a few couture cocktail dresses with décolletage and some new stilettos.

I have a photo of myself coming down the Stairs to Nowhere in the hotel.

I'm wearing a turquoise blue cocktail length satin dress with a flared skirt, like *The Seven Year Itch* costume, a high neck and a diamond cut out that reaches below the breast. Of course I am not wearing a bra. The spiked heels are dyed turquoise blue to match. How did we get shoes dyed so fast? And I have on elbow length leather white gloves.

Each time I look at that photo I hold my breath, worried I'll take a drunken fall to the marble floor of the lobby.

I spent much time at the pool lounging in a one-piece bathing suit, walking to and from the bar in gold sandals with kitten heels. I stocked up on the costume jewelry that Marilyn always wore and often rhinestones twinkled at my ears during the day. The stones I wore at night were real.

I was glamorous again, leaning on my comedienne skills.

I became a hanger-on with a group of New Yorkers. These were couples who were buying apartments in the city that were just turning co-op. The men were lawyers, doctors, stockbrokers. One was a judge. He was single and the others were always trying to put us together. He was very much the gentleman, too demure I remember thinking. Later I realized he must have been a gay man still closeted.

Morris Lapidus, the Fontainebleau architect, wanted the hotel to be excessive and he got his wish. I think there were seven restaurants and we never left the premises.

The fancy pants adored me. "Cherie, have dinner with us," or "Rodney Dangerfield is here tonight, please join us." Even "You must come back to New York with us!"

I don't know what I might have told them, but I bought a lot of dinners and drinks and kept the wives in stitches.

The spell was broken the night Frank Sinatra was booked. I had known Frankie was coming for the ten days I had been there, but I did what drunks do, put it out of my mind and drank some more. I missed Frankie so. What I would have done to see Frankie. The irony. And of course the New Yorkers were relentless: the judge asked me to be his guest; Missy, the loudest of the group made a reservation at the table with a place for me; the man I grew to despise, Steve, presented me with a ticket.

The day of Sinatra's gig I played sick. I called Steve and thanked him for the ticket but begged off with a migraine. Then I started drinking champagne with tequila chasers. By cocktail hour I had called the hotel doctor whose job it was to keep the guests happy and he prescribed phenobarbital and valium for the headache. At last my yearning to be close to my old friend and the youth and life I had left was thwarted.

The next morning, still drunk, I checked out and ran into Steve at breakfast. He was on his way to the Keys and asked me to accompany him. There was a chartered plane. I was aimless. This seemed like another adventure.

Big mistake.

My days began to brown out and stayed that way. There is not one entire 24-hour period that I can put together.

I do remember pieces.

I remember staying as a guest in a house on Pinder Lane that was owned by Seymour Lawrence, a book publisher. I'm not sure, but I think Steve was one of Lawrence's angels, because Lawrence was brilliant but his books were literary and not always commercially successful. Believe me, I knew about popular literature. Miller and I argued viciously about the lack of entertainment in *The Misfits*.

Anyway, you could tell right away that Steve Connelly was the kind of guy who liked to think of himself as a patron of the arts, a connoisseur. In other words, he was pretentious.

The host was not in residence but he gave us a memorable weekend just the same. The first afternoon we arrived a luncheon was thrown for us. In attendance were writers whose names were well known, and all of them, since this was Key West, homosexuals.

I played my rich drunken wannabe part quite well, I have to say, and the men were so egocentric that none of them looked long enough at me to wonder any further than my nose. Lawrence's fabulous Cuban maid served fresh conch salad and brisk white wine.

I was drinking champagne nonstop and I added other drugs into the mix I was already taking, this time marijuana and cocaine.

After dark, Steven and I swam naked in the outdoor pool. Steve wanted to show me off at the local clubs, but I resisted and he started asking why I insisted on isolating all the time.

He wanted crowds and nightclubs and one night he wanted anal sex. When I refused him he asked if he could pee on me instead. This is how far I had fallen.

I flashed back to the Marilyn party girl sleeping with leering older men at Johnny Hyde's house in order to get cast in movies. Now I was worse -- a lonely, drunken middle-aged whore sleeping with pretentious pricks so I wouldn't be alone.

But even that had limits.

I left Seymour Laurence's house. I was drunk, but not yet comatose. Even in the fugue state that was my existence I knew that there was always the threat of my being identified and I had to keep everything around me calm and collected. No dramas.

Here was a brief moment of clarity, all the more remarkable because it surfaced through my stupor.

Both Steve and I had rented cars so I could have "some girl time" is what I told him, so I drove off completely inebriated.

I'm sure there was a bottle of something or other to drink in the car. Driving under the influence was barely a traffic violation in those days.

I am certain by Marathon I was driving in a black out.

I don't know why I never killed anybody while I was driving. I hear often about people just like me who were not so lucky, average people who ran over children on bikes, drunks getting sober who admit to driving away after killing young moms out for a jog.

This and other terrible things I'd heard did not yet happen to me, and this is part of the reason I'm wondering if at eighty-five I should risk undergoing hours of complicated surgery and the anesthesia to repair my face, or if I should I just resign myself to my disfigurement. How much battering can a brain take before it cries uncle?

I left the car at the miniature Key West airport and flew to Tampa. The Spanish enclave drew me to it. Dinner at the Columbia restaurant was shared with a gentleman who asked me to join him. We shared fabulously unimportant conversation then took a stroll.

The Spanish man excused himself and I spent time watching the cigar makers. Even today, if you know where to look, Cuban cigar makers roll the exquisite tubes that filled humidors all over Hollywood when I was there. These luxury cigars were a fixture in the swanky studio offices and at the well-lubricated parties Marilyn attended as a starlet and I watched a dark pair of hands in the window of a shop daintily rolling the tobacco into a roll as luscious looking as an Italian cannoli. The cigars made me lonely for a life I had escaped, I was that desperate. So I kept running to avoid the pain.

This time back to the east coast of Florida, just driving and drinking. Also I was doctor shopping, cadging prescriptions for tranquilizers from doctors within my triangle: valium, seconal, definitely there was some Dexedrine in the mix.

I was spiraling downward, spending money, ignoring the letters forwarded from the offshore address the estate lawyer set up for Joe to a box I had opened in Miami before I left for Cuba, verifying that I was actually spending the funds that were leaving the account in such great amounts so quickly.

Other communication reaching me from that box was also ignored. I was on a slow suicide mission, isolating myself from anyone who had the slightest interest in my wellbeing.

Irving Miller sent me a birthday card. To this day I despise myself for ignoring Arthur's elderly father's note asking after my health, wanting nothing but a note to let him know I was OK.

Sue wrote twice a week at least, sometimes just a thought for the day. She knew I was in serious trouble but she could do nothing but throw a rope out and beseech me to grab on.

Joey wrote, first one letter and then another. Word reached me that Paula Strasberg was dying of cancer. I stopped going to the mail box.

I was fading into a ridiculous impersonation of myself. I was bloated, my face was blotchy.

It was late fall, 1963. I was 37 and cellulite was creeping down my thighs. I no longer combed my hair or had my nails done, rarely wore make-up. To be honest, I did not bathe all that much. I stunk so bad other people were veering away from me.

In a tiki bar near Marathon which is a little town right before the keys, I watched TV as Mr. and Mrs. Kennedy drove through Dallas in the open car. Shards of bitter resentment stabbed at my belly. I was drinking shots of whiskey. The wrinkled, stubble-faced charter boat captain seated next to me was trying to pick me up so he bought me another. "Down the hatch," we clicked glasses. Shots rang out. For one insane moment I believed my hateful thoughts had caused the shooting.

I asked the bartender to call me a cab. I haven't had a drink or a drug since that moment. John's death brought me Grace.

***

I had the cab bring me to a hospital close to where I knew there was recovery. I sobered up in an emergency room in Delray. I had not had a drink in many hours and was shaking, seeing things flitting beyond my peripheral vision. I believe the shaking would have led to convulsions but the admitting nurse gave me a Librium and put me at the head of the line. I figured she must have had some withdrawal in her time.

The fresh-faced doctor infuriated me because I was certain he had never had a drink in his life. My blood alcohol level must have come back really high because no one asked me any questions, they just put me right on a gurney. There were no rehabs back then, only drunk tanks and psych wards.

And there were the smoky rooms in church basements.

I refused admission to the psych ward. I would not go in the direction my mother or her mother or her mother's father did.

When I was stable enough to walk to a pay phone -- though I'm not sure you could call it walking, more like falling against the wall and dragging myself -- I called Sue.

Mercifully, she was there. Sue was always there.

I sure didn't know where I was staying, but my key chain said "Delmore Motel, Military Trail, Delray," and that was enough information. She called someone from the healing rooms in the Delray area who picked me up and got me where I had to go.

I detoxed in the smoky basements, staying in those healing rooms until I could eat and breathe. I slept in people's homes until I could trust myself not to drink and then I slept in Howard Johnson's.

At first I had tremors and convulsions. Without Librium to ease my craving for alcohol, I was in a sorry state. I longed for a lobotomy. Or electroshock therapy.

I didn't want to live if I couldn't have alcohol, but I didn't want to go on the way I had been, either. This sobering up was different than the last time, though. The craziness was flowing out of me and on the other side there was a real person, not a manufactured wet-dream, a chameleon, not a made-up anything.

Strangers surrounded and protected me, got me from one meeting to another, made me eat. There was always someplace to sleep.

If we witnessed the behavior of an alien entering our world I believe it would resemble something like recovering alcoholics. One alien comes into a room, despairing that he can't fit in society. The others who have been there provide him with all the tools he needs to prevail. They teach him how to feed, clothe and nurture himself, how to behave, to form relationships and have love affairs. The alien will always be the being he was inside but on the outside he will have learned to live among earthlings.

I was homeless but also rich. The house at Palm Drive was rented and that income went directly to the funds funneling through Joe. He kept control over my access to this money. He hated me but loved me still, and wanted some connection. I was under the impression that the money would never run out.

I was wrong.

NEW YORK, NEW YORK
1964-1967

I stayed in Delray "getting my head together" as I learned to say. I rented an apartment in a gated community and spent a lot of time around a small circle of people who were like me, I mean sober. I didn't know enough yet about the rest of me but I was learning.

Delray held most of its meetings in a building behind a strip club. They've moved now. But it was easy to find, just go down Military Trail to Jog Rd and look for the girly sign.

It was time for me to decide what I wanted to do. Acting wasn't even on the wish list. My education had been aborted and my brain was ravenous.

I had longed my whole acting career to perform Chekov, and not just in some scene study workshop at the Actors Studio. I loved Dostoyevsky and had tried to get a part in the Broadway production of *The Brothers Karamazov* but that's a story that ended badly. Tolstoy, Gorky, the Russian writers spoke to my blonde-haired, blue-eyed California soul.

Who knows why? I suspect it was the heavy-handed sorrow and constant brush with tragedy and the dark that drew me.

I wanted to go to school. And I wanted to live in New York. And since I would not be spending all my time at the Actors Studio or with the psychiatrist, Dr. Marianne Kris, the bitch who committed me to Payne Whitney, maybe I would get to see some of the place.

I settled on The New School because it seemed forward looking and more suited to my unconventional situation, older without a name.

I did not look for an apartment in Manhattan at first. The stimulus was still too much for my nerves which were not quite newborn but felt that way.

Forest Hills Garden was and still is an art deco enclave hidden behind the Long Island Railroad. The homes and apartment buildings in the Gardens lean towards brick arches, with ivy covered facades and stained glass windows. I found a rental in the paper without background and credit checks like people did back then and cocooned in a grand brick building with mahogany doors and marble floors then settled in for the first time in my life to a routine.

I was 41 years old and I had to call Sue to ask what I should buy to stock my refrigerator.

My growing up had been chaotic, and in Hollywood I had jumped from counting change in order to eat to being pampered by cooks and maids. Now I learned to live like an independent adult. I mothered myself. Learned to cook and separate the whites from the darks. Three times a week I attended a healing meeting either near the University or in Forest Hills.

Unfortunately most people now associate this neighborhood with the Son of Sam killings but when I lived there the US Open tennis match which is on the circuit with Wimbledon was held on courts at the Garden's tennis club. I attended the match once and saw Arthur Ashe, and Billie Jean King. God I'm a dinosaur and I better write this journal quick before I become endangered.

The food stand had Grey Poupon mustard which was exceptional for that time. And I would know. After all I had been married to an honored Yankee and considered myself a stadium food connoisseur.

At the New School I no longer worried about being recognized. Nobody paid any attention to me. The young men looked only at the gorgeous young women, with their braless tee shirts, and long, unadorned hair. I was regular, just older. I was quiet, because I am by nature quiet and shy.

At school, I learned just how good my brain is. All those years of being whispery and provocative and here I was finally finishing and polishing my mind.

My personal life consisted of going to the movies, often alone.

I have never lost my love affair with Hollywood, though that relationship has altered, grown less rabid like any love affair. I still see, or did until now, every important movie, though no one really "goes" to the movies anymore, including me.

What I say about the changes in the entertainment world will only add to the incessant chatter. Nothing will ever compare to my Hollywood but the '60s and '70s movies that used repertory groups of directors and actors brought art and entertainment together rather than keeping them as two separate things and movies thrived. Then something bad happened. Better minds then mine will have to trace the source. All I know is television did not ruin Hollywood. Hollywood showed contempt for the American audience and they left, feeling snubbed perhaps, which probably is why television keeps getting better. Talent migrated there.

As for social networks they (or should I say, it?) are too cold and intellectual to encourage a passionate attachment. We are all doomed, moving closer to our own ideas of alien creatures.

Anyway, the movies and a few inconsequential romances and female friends met through my meetings defined my life. I was safe with these people. No one said "Let's meet for drinks" or ordered wine with dinner or threw parties with bartenders in white jackets or coolers with kegs. I was safe in every way with my people. All alcoholics have contorted themselves to hide their compulsion from anyone close to them. I did not seem so queer to this circle. Everyone I knew was marked by a bit of a twist in their thinking.

Inside me a different story was going on. About the time I was beginning to take Master's level classes, my circumscribed life started to get old. The Russians could keep me satisfied for just so long. Furthermore, a life of predictable routine might be the best thing for me, but I was not healed enough yet to know that. I still needed at least a *little* drama. How could I have expected to go from who and where I had been to Queens and stay there long?

AFTER THE FALL
1968-1972

I met Reggie at the Mustard Seed, a meeting established in the early years of the NY rooms on 3rd Ave and 23rd St.

I was maybe twenty years his senior. I did not take exams since I was not a registered student, but I awarded myself a Masters all the same. Quite a step up for me in the self-esteem department.

Awarding it, I mean.

It was a beautiful June evening. He was standing near the butt can but not smoking. Later he would tell me that he appreciated that I was not trying to pass for a co-ed, like so many of the older women were doing then, wearing miniskirts and peasant blouses. Nor was I thin. He referred to me in those early days as curvaceous, a word that people didn't use anymore. We were looking at each other across the crowd. Later he would tell me that what he was thinking was, "Either I'm crazy or that's Marilyn Monroe."

Reggie was ten when Monroe died, and he never tired of telling me that *his* blonde was Debby Harry.

In all the time we were together I never told Reggie who I was.

I still wonder if knowing he had been Marilyn's young lover would have made him love himself a little more.

He followed a few feet behind me as the group broke up after the 8:00PM meeting. I let him catch up and walk me the twenty blocks or so to the Chelsea Hotel, where I had moved and was practicing being a Bohemian.

Just one more identity to add to my repertoire of white-trash foster child, orphan, wife, pin-up, sex-for-parts starlet, sex kitten, wife, drug addict, wife, sex goddess, drunk, dead, recovering drunk, and middle-aged college student.

We sat in the lobby. I gave him the same story I told everyone—I was clean over two years, getting a late education in Russian literature--had been an actress until I hit bottom.

Into the late night we exchanged our stories. I had a new voice then. I've evolved from it now but I believe it was slightly southern.

Around midnight, Gray, the concierge, if you could call him that, at the switchboard leaned out of his cubbyhole and said, "Call for you. Want it here?"

Nothing about the way Gray said it made me think I needed to rush over.

I took my time, giving Reggie a chance to check me from behind. This *tete-a-tete* had started out kosher. I was old enough to be his mother, or maybe a younger aunt.

But it was apparent it could become something else..

Sue spoke. I disbelieved my ears.

The small transistor radio the old man was playing at the switchboard was tuned to an all-news station and I assumed the broadcast was about Bobby Kennedy winning the nomination. I noted a group of people entering and heard *Robert Kennedy, hotel, kitchen, shot.*

The truth pierced my brain. Reggie was standing; it looked like he was leaving. The empty space inside me was screaming for help in blocking out the memories. Instinct drove me toward the door, and I grabbed onto his sleeve.

"Did you hear?" I was crying, and so was he. We just held on tight. Strangers all over the lobby were comforting each other.

It was past midnight and I had a small television in my room so we went upstairs to watch and mourn. I especially did not want to be alone because my fingers itched to call one of the Lawfords or the other people Marilyn knew close to the Kennedy clan.

Jack's assassination had triggered my getting sober. I was superstitious. I didn't want Bobby's death to be a bookend to that.

Upstairs, I called Sue back from the marble tiled bathroom in the kitchenette suite that was my home at the Chelsea.

"What more have you heard?"

"Do you mean about the Senator?"

"Yes, well what else?"

Sue did not know the names of my lovers but she had more information than anyone else who knew I was alive.   I so wanted to tell her of how special Bobby had been,

To tell her of his intuitive compassion for the dreadful loneliness that consumed me, the zeal he had for all of life that so often lifted me from despair. I yearned to tell her the special grief that I thought was mine.

There was a pause long enough to tell me Sue was putting together another piece of the puzzle. She was so delicate as she spoke to my clawing need.

"He was so young, and all those children. We all have to be grateful that Mrs. Kennedy shared him with us at all."

God bless that woman, she plunked me right back to the ground. I hung up, checked my lipstick. Reggie asked to use the phone to call one of his own sober friends -- we were slipping easily into our parts.

***

I suspect the circumstances enhanced our empathy for each other and that grew into passion.

We comforted each other through the next days. Once I pushed my ego aside I realized it did not matter that Bobby had been a close friend; everyone had lost an irreplaceable and cherished piece of the fabric of our history. Reggie talked a lot about the Kennedy tragedy feeling personal. There were spontaneous vigils all over the city; the rooms were packed because drunks knew to fortify themselves. Reggie and I attached to each other. It just seemed natural.

Oddly we didn't sleep together for weeks. I was much too raw to be touched, my way of mourning, and he either sensed that or had a similar feeling. I never asked him if he worked or how he supported himself. I knew he was a musician but seemed to have no gigs or other responsibilities.

This was so common then in the healing rooms that I didn't consider it strange.

He basically moved his guitar and a few pair of jeans into my room at the hotel. He didn't even need a drawer for his underwear. Like Marilyn, he went commando, though I did not know the word until he taught it to me. I was so glad someone was there. Some might say that for me, Reggie was convenient.

It did not occur to me that Reggie might have a say in what happened between us. I was not making very good decisions. For example, I left him for dead in Rome, and that was wrong.

When John was assassinated I had been propelled into a second journey of recovery which is by nature all-consuming so Bobby's death did double duty. I had made up fairy tales about the Kennedys and then reviled both brothers when those tales turned out to be dreams. Now I was looking back with shame at what a drunken fool I must have seemed to these men and how I debased myself. I despaired that I had lost the opportunity to redeem myself in their eyes.

And now, The Marilyn Monroe "alleged" suicide came back as fodder for the tabloids. My death was conflated with the assassinations and words like homicide and conspiracy were tossed around. Truthfully it is possible there was some connection. I have no idea. It is feasible that Important People pulled strings when it was decided that I would be pronounced dead. The disappearing was my decision, but whomever helped the original disinformation is secret even from me. I had wondered when I first got conscious what questions to ask and decided the less I knew about who knew what and how, the better.

I'm not saying anyone outside of the DiMaggios was involved. I am only saying that cover ups and conspiracies were like family events back then. It was easy to coalesce around a hurting member and make something happen. In those days the circle of players was very small. If you went to a Hollywood party, you probably sat next to someone in the Cabinet and reached him on the telephone the next day. In fact, that is exactly how Bobby and I became friendly. I knew he would be at a dinner party at the Lawfords, so I asked Irving Miller for some good questions to make conversation. I actually brought notes in my evening bag. Consequently Bobby and I talked about civil rights for hours. When I called his office, he got right on the phone.

Jack was different. He spent a weekend with me and then never again took my calls. Of course, I understand all of it now. I was, at the end, a drunk and crazy to boot, no different than Frances Farmer right before her mother had her lobotomized. Some people in fact would have been better off if I weren't in a position to talk about them, but that doesn't mean they wanted to kill me.

Anyway, the Congress was discussing putting together another committee to examine the assassinations since the Warren Commission's one gunman theory had been derided. Don't forget Martin Luther King Jr. had also been gunned down that year. The Republicans had to at least pretend to do something.

When I examined the situation from this angle it was obvious I had to move on. More than enough people saw me on a daily basis and though they were ethically bound to protect my anonymity you could only trust people so far. And not very far at that was my experience.

Once more I asked myself if I should return to the world, announce that I was not dead, and pick up my place again. But Marilyn Monroe had been supplanted by gorgeous performers like Meryl Streep and, Jessica Lange, blondes who could be funny and serious at the same time with no one wondering if they could do both.

Maybe I could do something else for a living, get my degree for real, and write a dissertation on the semiotics of shadow in War and Peace then get a tenured job somewhere. Or go into politics.

I took a good look in the mirror and got an answer.

Even disguised, the creature still consumed me. I had yet to shed her. One step into the real world and Monroe would be snapped up, a has-been supported by book deals and talk shows. She would trample the self I had been fighting to discover, and it wouldn't even be her fault. Until I either died or killed her I was destined to remain undercover. All of us who had devised Marilyn Monroe had done our jobs too well—Marilyn, the creature, lived on.

***

Now I needed ID. This involved calling on the mafia connections that really did lurk between me and Mr. Kennedy rather than the ones FBI Director Herbert Hoover manufactured and planted agents to verify.

Sam Giancana was an old friend of mine via Sinatra. Frank and I had been roommates in his house in Malibu and though people said we were an item, we did not become lovers in the Malibu house. He was still mourning Ava Gardner.

For the record he did not "share" me with anyone. He had enough *tsuris* keeping happy the two long term mistresses he already had. Sam was like a big stuffed Mamma bear, very sweet if he didn't have a beef against you. Also, Sam and his ilk were used to people disappearing and not apt to talk about it.

He put me in touch with a guy named Milo in New York. I'm not making this up. It was like something straight out of one of those gangster movies Jimmy Cagney made. Pacino made them later, and now the Latino actors and African American actors make them. The studios wither and die but movies never change. Anyway, Milo met me at The Palm on Second Avenue.

He was a broad shouldered man on the hefty side. Short. He wore a handmade Italian suit which made him stand out, since the crowd was casual. The Palm has hand drawn caricatures all over the walls, and when I was taken to our table, I noticed Mayor Lindsay had been added. Poor John Lindsay was just the wrong mayor for New York City, WASPish and much too polished for the ethnic characters that enrich the boroughs and derided his manicured ways.

All through the transaction Milo was staring at me, and not in a good way. I mentioned Sam a few times, what good friends we were. He wasn't listening. He gave me the papers and I gave him $2,500. He finished his martini and I finished my Tab.

There was a stretch limo double-parked on Second Avenue. The fat little man offered me a lift and I politely refused. When he grabbed me and tried to pull me into the car, I was grateful for all those years I had spent lifting dumbbells before it was fashionable.

Before his driver pulled away, he let me know that I wasn't fooling anybody and he would find a way to get back at me for disrespecting him. *"Cherie Stoppard* is your name like I'm Dwight Eisenhower," he yelled after me. If he found me, this guy was definitely going to make trouble.

ST. ALBANS MEMORIAL HOSPITAL
Portland, Oregon, 2011

The afternoon goes by slowly while doctors decide my fate. There are considerations for a woman of my age. Will I survive the surgery? Die of infection? I have seen many brilliant elderly people go under anesthesia only to recover physically with their minds undone. I suspect many of my peers diagnosed with dementia are victims of drug mishaps under the knife. I would rather die just the way I am now than lose my marbles.

Few people mourned Marilyn. DiMaggio disallowed any Hollywood people to attend the funeral. If I die now there will be hundreds who come to pay their respects to Cherie. So who did Joey snatch back to life?

My existence is a conundrum. I have spent 85 years spelunking through the cave that is me, planting flags where I discover parts to claim for myself. The names Marilyn Monroe and Norma Jean don't even belong to me anymore. They are owned by a big conglomerate these days. Am I Tom Ewell's Girl or this old woman; the comedienne or the man killer? The drunk, the believer, the cougar, the lover of men, I am all of them. I am much more than them.

Cherie comes to say good bye as her shift is ending. She leans over the chair where I can now be seated in the solarium. I hug her, hold her longer than usual, wish her 'safe home.' She says, "Same to you." We both laugh a little. Where can I possibly be going?

ROMAN HOLIDAY
1970-1978

By the time I got everything together to leave the States it was 1970. I was 44. I was beginning to shed the piece of Marilyn that drew toward darkness. That meant I rose a bit from the pit which informed some of my later characters. People thought I was nothing but big bosoms and hips, and the less enlightened part of the audience never saw the intense work going on. I had turned down the part of Anna Freud right after making *The Misfits* only because my analyst asked me to.

That was one of my greatest regrets. I had turned myself inside out in psychoanalysis and then I had turned over my psyche to a shrink who went on to talk me out of my most creative intuitions. No wonder I committed suicide! Maybe we all make the mistake of sending out signals that distort who we are and sabotage our destiny.

A perfect example, the rejection that drove me ultimately toward the Russians came about in 1956.

At that time I was determined to play the part of Grushenka in Dostoyevsky's the Brothers Karamazov if I could get someone to audition me for the part. The Hollywood Reporter confirmed this rumor. I remember precisely the moment I turned away from this long-lived dream.

It was at a dinner given in my honor the night we finished shooting *The Seven Year Itch*.

Billy Wilder and I were dancing. I had not danced for so long, not since Joe and I were married, and now that we were divorcing it was heaven to move again.

I felt as bright as the rhinestones in my ears and on my wrists. I was airy -- drunk on champagne and stoned on pills, but not yet sluggish.

Billy danced me into a corner of the Trocadero and at first I thought he was going to kiss me. He put his hand in the pocket of his pants so perhaps it was a congratulations present.

We were destined to kill every other studio at the box office.

Instead he bent down and whispered, and I will never forget his words, "Baby, give up the Russian."

At first I didn't catch his meaning. Instead I laughed. The booze put me a second or two behind real time. Then I understood. "No – I want that part. Paula and I have started reading lines."

(Paula Strasberg was my coach and Wilder's nemesis but that's a different story.)

"Baby, trust me."

"Billy what does it mean when a Hollywood agent says, *Trust me*?" This joke was old even then.

At this point, I was needing another drink really bad. There was a blackbird or two in my purse. I started to open it and Billy put his hand over mine. "Marilyn, everyone is making fun of you. You'll only end up heart broken. Don't make a fool of yourself."

Don't make a worse fool of yourself is what he meant. At that point I had made my mark in the business of Hollywood but there were many just like Daryl Zanuck and most of 20th Century Fox who considered me a joke and a freak, a moron, a whore.

My voice was still Marilyn's in those days and no one ever knew what I was masking, the feelings beneath The Girl's pretty bottom and hot smile. But I knew. At that moment I decided Hollywood could say goodbye to Marilyn. My sense of self was the fragile shell of a sunflower seed. But the one thing I could do was kill Marilyn. I was six years away from my "suicide."

***

I did always love Russian literature so when Reggie and I were leaving, Russia would have been my choice for a home, but it was not easy to get there.

London was the center of the universe and I was avoiding crowds.

I chose Rome.

Once there I started wearing bell bottoms and a suede jacket with fringe and carrying a back pack. Reg came with me. He was a blithe spirit. He was searching, I was searching, he was broke, I was not. He mellowed out my days and satisfied my nights. So I was having my sexual revolution. I was playful. The world was sweet. I was coming closer to feeling at home in myself.

Rome had an opening in an orphanage for a low level job, a teacher's assistant for their pre-schoolers. I only needed to speak as much Italian as the toddlers so I crashed an Italian course and went to work. It was amazing what I could accomplish without the pressure of people watching and directing, wanting things from me. The babies loved me. I began to love me. I grew my hair. I was going grey and I let it be. American women my age tortured themselves to stay thin, but not me. I was built like a brick shithouse. Reg played his guitar in Vatican City. He began to call me Marilyn. It was his nickname for me. To his dying day he never learned who I was.

And there were those smoky rooms here, of course; they were everywhere, saving me, holding me. The craving to obliterate myself had gone and I was filling up the hollow it left with peace and self and God, yes, God. Later on, I would go behind the Marilyn mask and I found God.

***

Joe located me. I had purposefully left no word with anyone but Sue, and he frightened her into telling him by threatening to reveal her affair with Marguerite Mann. That would have been no problem for Sue, but Mann had been closeted, married, and by this point a staunch example of sobriety and to reveal her sexual proclivities would be to threaten or even topple the only system that was actually healing drunks.

For all the "free love" in the sexual revolution, there was still way too much fear of lesbians. Sue could not risk it. But she did not tell him about Reg.

We moved immediately to Spain, but I kept asking myself, who was I running from?

We traveled through Northern Spain following the pilgrims' path to Santiago deCompostella where I got drunk on the cheese because it was so heady. A reporter from an entertainment newspaper had discovered Reg and he had a small fan base growing.

I knew much about promotion and I took out ads in small newspapers ahead of our journey and got him into a few cafes.

Everyone hated Americans because of the Vietnam War, but Reg's music was agitprop, so he was popular among the U. S. kids on tour as well as the Spaniards.

He was growing up.

I didn't see his betrayal coming.

I faced down Joe in Barcelona. The Spanish eat dinner very late, eleven PM, maybe midnight. I never got used to their Mediterranean culture and was invariably in bed by 10, having eaten crackers and sardines from a can. Reg and I lived in hotels.

In Barcelona there was an old monastery that had been turned into a parador. Every room had mammoth windows that opened onto a cobblestone courtyard where the monks must have meditated. I know I did.

Anyway, this is where I met with Joe. It was dinnertime for most of Spain. Reg was playing at a café near the town square. Joe had the front desk call me down and we went out to the courtyard. Spain's night sky varies depending on where you are. Near the Basque country, the mountains mix with the moon shadows. Barcelona has a navy blue sky with no stars. A city sky.

We talked a great deal about Joey, who was deep into his addiction and living in a box on the streets of New York City.

DiMaggio had given up on him. There was no point in having the conversation about disease versus willpower because Joe was never going to accept his child so long as he showed a weakness for drugs and alcohol. Joe could not abide anything he did not control or intimidate and he was not going to intimidate alcoholism no matter what he did to Joey.

His need to control was exactly why he never really stopped fighting the battle to win me back. He could not accept that I was directed by something much more powerful than him, call it spirit, and he couldn't control the force driving me, my soul's ecstatic passion to prevail.

Come home, he was saying, let the world know you're still here. I did consider whether or not I should return to New York to see if I could help Joey. I owed him the living I was doing so peacefully and with such joy. The change in my psyche by then was enough for me to know that no booze, pill or psychiatrist could save me. What stopped the noise in my head was soothing someone else.

Maybe it was the ghosts of all those meditating monks but I came to my senses and realized I could not give in. Joe's suggestion only enhanced my rationalization for staying under the radar. People would expect me to be who I was and I could not be young and beautiful anymore. There would be too many expectations. I would not be allowed to be myself.

There would be no more parts for me and I would feel rejected and devastated. As for helping Joey, I would make calls to New York and have other people reach out to him on the streets and see if we could get him back to sanity. As I have written, there was a system in place, the friends he did not know yet would help him.

As for returning to being Marilyn Monroe -- looking back, I realize I could have used her. She could have been a role model for every woman my age who was finally embracing her orgasms and her sisters, letting her breasts go free, getting an education, a job, a female lover. I could have made a statement. But I sent Joe away without Marilyn and with the edict that he was not to look for me anymore. There was a boy twenty or more years his junior in my life, a real lover boy, I said, just to drive the point home. And Joe never looked for me again.

But he never stopped wooing me — to wit, the flowers he sent all of his life to the mausoleum that he knew was empty. As for that mausoleum, I do feel sorry for the Japanese gentleman who paid 4.6 million dollars for the plot next to mine. He's going to be ticked off when he reads that my body isn't there.

***

Two nights after Joe's visit the manager of the club where Joey was appearing called and asked me to come get Reggie.

"Pick him up? I have no scooter, nothing. He has it."

"Then take a taxi. There's an accident."

"Is he hurt?"

"Si. Bring a taxi."

Why didn't they call an ambulance? The question did not occur to me until I was on my way. Reg had overdosed on heroin, that's why. We had maintained our sobriety together for five years – or I thought we had – and I was devastated, blindsided. I'd never seen it coming. Maybe I shouldn't say that Reg betrayed me. I should say I felt betrayed. In the ambulance the medics placed an oxygen mask over his face, but the gruesome expression in the lead medic's black eyes told me everything I needed to know. End of story. At the hospital, Reggie was put on a gurney and taken away.

I hesitated for a day or two about what to do for Reggie's remains. Finally I called the hospital, but the volunteer I was transferred to who spoke English insisted that there was no unclaimed body of an American in the morgue. Perhaps he had already been taken away. Reggie's family was as dysfunctional as any other, and though they'd more or less disowned him, they wouldn't be hard to track down. Any competent official at the American Embassy could have contacted one of them. So I called the American Embassy, gave them Reg's name, and told them I wanted to either claim the body or know what happened to it, but when they asked for my name and my relationship to him,

I hung up. It suddenly became obvious that if I started asking questions, the embassy workers might just start asking questions of their own. And if I talked to the constabularies – no, I couldn't do that. Drugs had been involved.

I was sick with indecision, and on top of that, grief. Finally, I realized there was nothing more I could do for Reggie.

No matter how you look at it, I abandoned him there, me who spent so many hours on couches wailing and whining about being left behind.

The end result was that, like Ed Digby, the car dealer in Northern California, this experience with Reggie would teach me about consequences, but that came later.

DETOUR
Marbella, 1976

I couldn't go home. The U.S. Select Committee on Assassinations was in full throttle and The Monroe/Kennedy/Mafia connection was on the table. I decided I was to stay a fugitive, or an ex-pat, living under an alias in a foreign country for a few years to come.

I am not sure why I veered south. I knew that Igor Cassini, the funny little Russian gossip columnist who wrote *Ask Cholly*, had a villa on the Mediterranean close to the harbor facing Africa, and that he had started renting it out to tourists. Maybe that explains it.

Right near Igor's villa was a small café though technically everything was near everything else. And everyone knew everyone else. So the moment I walked into The America Café the two guys at the bar and group of four dining early turned and gestured hellos.

The waitress with the aqua eyes came to my table to hand me a menu and within five minutes I knew all about her. Melanie was a tall, graceful Dutch torch singer making a name for herself in the small Spanish province.

I could not see her without imagining tulips, for such was the shape of her face surrounded by auburn hair hennaed a bit red and shaped with shags to her chin, balanced on her graceful neck like the flower on its stem.

The food at the café was *mens a mens* to be sure but the company was nice for a stranger in a strange place. I had not been alone in quite some time and was very nervous about maintaining my sobriety. No meetings took place here. My waitress become my guide, my companion, and then my lover. Her irrepressible smile made her face bloom, and the way her eyes brightened when she saw me, was like bathing in the warm Mediterranean sea. In fact when I remember her it is always standing at the harbor club on the docks near the sea.

Our affair was experimental on my part. We were listening to blues in the upstairs bedroom of the Cassini home. I hated the floor downstairs because there was a portrait of Mrs. Cassini hanging over the dining room table and in truth, she had a kind of sour look around her mouth that made me squirm. So I slept in a guest room upstairs.

We were probably listening to Ella Fitzgerald or Billie Holiday. I would not listen to Sinatra, it was too painful. And who was listening to Sinatra anymore? I did not know that Melanie loved women.

She was dancing alone, so I reached out my hand and we danced, two women, wearing jeans and tee shirts, bare foot, no make-up, totally natural. It was all so natural.

When she kissed my eyebrow, then the mole, OK the beauty mark, on my cheek, I became conscious.

"Melanie." I was going to tell her I was a virgin so far as lesbian love was concerned but her touch on my thigh moved between my legs and I was paralyzed with longing, wet in a way I had not been ever for Reggie. Then we were lying down.

That's what I know about that one hour. She didn't need to teach me much. Afterwards, we sat up, my jeans hanging on one leg, her panties pulled down to her knees,

"Never done this." I was blushing.

"This I don't believe." Her accent made even hard consonants sound tender. A little like the Cubans actually. Maybe only Americans and the Brits speak like they are mashing words.

So we did it again. And often. But I grew tired of it and there is nothing nice to say about what I did. I wasn't gay. I loved men. I had seen everything there was to see of Marbella and my rental was up. I wanted to leave.

I made a reservation at a place where tourists went so she would feel spoiled. She asked if we could order a bottle of wine for dinner. This is when I told her I was an alcoholic. My horrible thought was perhaps that would push her away.

I wondered why you never drink like others from Europe was all she said. I simply reminded her I was American.

The things we did not know about each other were more glaring that night than any other.

I had seen her perform but my standards for torch singers were very high and she could never meet them. Or, and this is the worst truth, I would never have let her meet them so I could have reason not to know her.

Too much analysis is a very dangerous thing.

At the end of the meal we went down to the harbor and I held her while I told her I had a plane ticket back to Rome the next morning. For the very first time in my life I was playing the man. That is, I was stoic, I stayed cool. She wept in my arms. We agreed to stay in touch and perhaps I would come back in the winter. We never corresponded again.

I am ashamed of how I used her. I knew no other way; I had been trained by masters. Think of my foster parents marrying me off to Dougherty because my last foster father wanted to abuse me or Arthur announcing to the HUAA that he was marrying America's Sweetheart WITHOUT BOTHERING TO ASK ME, knowing the senators would ease up on Marilyn's husband. I am hoping that what I did to Melanie is the end game in a long line of abuse at the hands of users.

I apologize to you, Melanie, in public. Your iridescent presence, the shimmering sexuality you taught me that can only go on between women, was integral to my moving on. Wherever life took you after I ended our affair, I hope it was better for having known me.

So, now you know who I am, not the blonde, American, virgin lesbian, but Marilyn Monroe building a new self-image. I am so sorry that I hurt you.

This is treacherous, this memoir, because now I want to search for you to make amends. If I get through this procedure intact, that is exactly what I am going to do-hire one of those detectives from the internet.

I thought I moved through life after Marilyn with grace and stealth but wherever I went I took me along. I thought I was evolving, but what I did to Melanie was no different than the hurt I caused Ed Digby back in the beginning or the unforgiveable act of leaving a lover's body all alone.

I have learned the best I can do is to live each day without hurting anyone including myself. Seems simple enough but try it sometime. Harder than Grushenka, that's for sure.

IF THIS IS TUESDAY,
THIS MUST BE...
Florence, 1978 - 1980

The Italians had begun an English speaking meeting in Florence. I flew back to Rome and stayed for a few days on my way to Tuscany.

The Sistine Chapel practically put me into a trance. The artist inside me stuck her head out from the soil and began to seek the sun. Suddenly I needed to inhabit another woman and act out her story instead of staying in my own.

This was my second visit and now I stayed for hours. In particular, I focused on the hand of God *not quite* touching Adam. The *not quite* stuck with me. *Nothing is perfect* it said to me.

Not even God's touch.

The English-speaking meeting in Florence saved me. I spoke to the women there about how they stayed away from alcohol when they could not control the crawling beneath the skin.

"I pray," someone said.

"I meditate" said another.

"I eat ice cream." This from an American student. That sounded like the best idea, so I found a gelato stand and spent a lot of time there.

It seemed like the Medicis owned half the real estate in Florence.

Across from my hotel was one of their homes with a gargoyle atop an iron gate guarding the entrance to the stone villa. It reminded me, in a certain way, of an old brownstone in Manhattan, though the Medici residence seemed to emanate a kind of decadence or underworldliness.

I didn't need an advanced history degree to sense the corruption that seemed to hover around the center of the city. In August Italy is hot. The cobblestones hurt my feet because I was wearing sandals, so I went to Tod and bought gold driving shoes. That was when I realized I could shop to chase away my hunger.

Everything I ever wanted was in Florence. Leather and jewels and high fashion by designers I had only read about. People didn't realize that I never owned any clothes. In my Marilyn life all I owned was the black mink Joe gave me and some Capri pants, pedal pushers we used to call them. When I needed a dress I would go to Twentieth Century's costume department and one of the seamstresses would sew me into something. That sequined dress in which Marilyn sang Happy Birthday to the president almost didn't make it. It was too tight. But when I was in Florence, I was in shape. Going without booze will do that for you, even if you eat a lot of gelato. People don't realize how small I was. Put me next to, Beyonce, let's say, and I will look like a ballet dancer next to a lady wrestler. Anyway, I was looking good. The June just past I had turned fifty-two.

One day I went back to my hotel and the clerk said he had a message for me. The lawyer who liaised with the bank had been trying to reach me by mail, as was our agreement, but I hadn't been great about getting back to him. If he called it was serious, and it was:

Cherie Stoppard and Gladys's fund were going broke

This never would have happened, of course, if I died when I was supposed to.

Unfortunately, two of us were living on the money Marilyn had left behind. The fancy sanitarium Mother called home most of the time was costing more than I had budgeted for in the trust.

Now there was about a year's worth of cash left for the two of us. I would have to place Gladys in a less expensive home.

That was painful. For a moment I wondered if this was cruel. After all, if nothing else, Mother and I were bound together in that borderline personality business. No matter that she had not nurtured me, she was and always would be Mother.

And we both wore costumes.

Gladys liked to dress in nurse uniforms. I can relate to that.

Many times I have worn costumes to pass as a normal person myself. So placing her in a home that was below my standards was difficult.

Would I end up in a place below my standards?

Then I realized that what had become a standard had profoundly changed for me and it had nothing to do with whatever would inevitably replace that fancy Westwood mausoleum. Take a look at that place sometime if you can. My fans have endowed me with their loving hands on my stone, flowers, messages. I am sorry I don't lie there, my friends, but this is better--I am actually here.

The royalties from my promotional image in *The Seven Year Itch* were accumulating, all those items you see with my white dress up. This is what Mother and I had to live on and not enough had yet accumulated. Not for a life spent shopping in Florence for me and Rockhaven for her.

I took the elevator up to my room on the fifth floor of the five-star hotel and stared out at the throngs below. All of them had a way to support themselves. People all over the world got up each day and earned their daily bread. It could not be beyond my reach.

As Marilyn, people assumed I made very few decisions, that I was like one of those wrought-iron silhouettes of cowboys people lean against their little houses with nothing behind them. But this had never been true. I had pushed around Daryl Zanuck, who despised me and considered me a freak. I worked my way up from a $75.00 per week contract to $100,000 a movie and then I began my own production company, MM Productions. Back then actresses just did not do that!

I might have made it seem that I was the victim of decisions early on before I got famous, but in fact, I was a slave to substances only, and then only after I became a celebrity.

So, how to get by until the promo money caught up? I called my anchor and guardian angel, Sue. We mulled it over and it was clear the best thing for me to do would be to settle my hotel bill, raise some cash, and get back to the States.

I didn't know what a middle-aged broken-down blonde might do to stir up income but it wasn't going to happen in Florence.

I flew back to Rome on my way to the States.

Near the Coliseum was a terrible neighborhood where if I had wanted drugs, they would have been plentiful. This might seem like a good neighborhood for me to avoid, but it had one big draw: plenty of pawn shops. I sold all the gold jewelry I had purchased when I was living it up as an addict, and when I'd discovered in Florence that it was also fun to shop.

Of course none of my own pieces would be available, since I was under the misconception that Lee Strasberg had distributed my property among my friends.

I would know better as time went on.

Some of the pieces I sold at the Coliseum I didn't even recognize. I'd apparently purchased them in a blackout.

I discovered these in the safety deposit box in Banca Nationala on Via Veneto where I plunked a satin bag of jewels that I had not had the heart at the time to explore. There was a platinum eternity ring from Harry Winston, but good sense prevailed and I opted to keep it for sale to a different type of merchant. And there were quite a few pair of ruby earrings that I also kept.

But there was a gold Piaget watch, 18k gold cuffs, brooch of a pooch, these I did not remember buying, but received about fifteen thousand dollars. The jewelry I bought in Florence brought me another fifteen thousand American dollars, (I insisted on American because once, long ago, the dollar was strong.) I got thirty thousand dollars for all the stuff, probably one fourth of what I had spent, but it didn't faze me.

Overnight it had struck me. I yearned to go home.

***

I had never done anything but work in a munitions factory, pose as a pin-up girl, and sell my soul. At age fifty-five, I didn't see myself as an ideal candidate for making guns or modeling half-naked for calendar shots. .

And, thank God, I was no longer able to sell my soul.

It just wasn't going to happen. This left me with no marketable skills

. I thought briefly about turning to Joe, but my affair with Melanie had made me take a good look at how I handled other people's feelings, and it was not with grace. "Do Unto Others" might seem trite or old-fashioned, but that is exactly what I was learning to do: follow The Golden Rule. I was hesitantly gluing the shards of myself together and being a good person seemed a good one to add to the mosaic.

SUNSET BOULEVARD
Hollywood. 1981

When I returned to the States from Rome it was real clear to me that the earth was scorching. You could live with the earthquakes but no one ever talked about the fires. Not in my memory.

I didn't remember Southern California being so hot, not when I was young and not when I left in 1962. I had been away for the Watts Riot of '64 and I sat out what in retrospect seems like the beginning of random evil let loose and never tamed, murders like Tate/Bianca and the upside-down abduction of Patty Hearst.

When I arrived it was obvious to me there was a new beat. There was a simmering, The difference between the Hollywood lifestyle and South LA was unnatural except in the way they were the same: everyone was doing dangerous drugs.

Something bad was going to happen.

I'm telling you, Los Angeles was set up for a conflagration. And these were just the man-made fires.

The forest fires that boomeranged into the luxury neighborhoods, Malibu, Santa Barbara, Brentwood, were not new.

Once Mother and I had climbed into her car when a fire went out of control in Beverly Hills and we drove all the way to the top. I was five, maybe.

She was visiting me at my foster parents' home, out of the hospital for the weekend. She said she was taking me to meet my father.

At the top of Sunset Boulevard, a fireman turned us around. Mother turned as frenzied and scathing as the flames licking up the neighborhood. You never knew what she was capable of doing in those moods. I wanted to yell to the fireman for help. I wanted to crawl beneath his yellow rubber coat and beg for safety and security. All of the time with her felt like that – I was in the midst of chaos and desperately seeking either escape or rescue.

***

They say only the good die young but what I think that means is if you look good when you die, people think of you kindly.

Returning home as a middle aged, middle class woman, average in every way was not an experience I would want to repeat.

Jim Morrison, Jimi Hendrix, Janis Joplin, Elvis—now I was just one of many beautiful young dead icons.

If I had appeared on the Hollywood scene in 1981 I would never have gotten a job, never mind become an icon.

And I mean, not even a waitressing job. Not in Hollywood.

My jeans were too tight in the waist and my jowls were slumping.

Without the black liquid eyeliner and multiple false eye lashes I looked like any middle-aged woman who didn't belong among the emerging Boomer phantasmagoria. There was no problem getting around. I did get Little Baby Jane Fonda's exercise tape because I was not going to be doing a whole lot of walking in LA, and I got really fit, enough to get into a unitard, I had let my hair go grey, it was that nice salt and pepper grey, but no one is grey in Hollywood, no one I've seen, maybe Helen Mirren and Michael Douglas, but no one else, so I dyed it back to honey blonde and I started wearing it in a kind of bob. I kept away from mirrors to avoid seeing the jowls. Even if I had the money, plastic surgery would have been too problematic.

I had always been in touch with Sue but when I went to see her I was shocked. It had not occurred to me that she was elderly. When the door opened and I saw her seated in her wheelchair I lost my bearings.

She was living in a horrible assisted-living home in La Brea. Her children had let her back into their lives many years before, when she had stopped drinking, but they had never really forgiven her for the damage alcoholism had caused the family.

She was getting too old to get herself to meetings but a group of people came to her on a weekly basis.

She wasn't alone..

But God she was lonely.

Mostly it seemed she remembered. That's how she spent her time, regretting her drinking days as a young mother and reflecting on the years she was first on a pink cloud as she got sober. This was the woman who had saved my life a number of times with just her voice over the telephone -- it was not an exaggeration to say so -- and now I was powerless to help her.

Or was I? The idea of how to help Sue did not come to me overnight. I'm a love-at-first sight kind of woman, but rational decisions take me time.

Though she would never take any of the money I had offered over the years, gift cards seemed to be acceptable, so over time I sent her all different kinds. For all I know, they remained in stacks on her night table near her oxygen tank, but I felt relieved, which just goes to show you that when you do something for somebody it's never certain who is getting the most benefit.

Also I was still receiving small royalties from that ridiculous book about me, *My Story*, ghostwritten by Ben Hecht, which he had no right to publish now that I was dead. He waited a year after I died, or she died, and then pop, there's a Marilyn Monroe "autobiography" on the stands.

No one ever knew where the royalties went because Hecht died before the book came out and his family could not penetrate the publisher.

So here's the answer. I got them.

And even twenty years later, the lawyer was still getting a few thousand dollars every six months. Now these checks were directed to Sue's bank account.

When I first returned I was staying at the Chateau Marmont, cheap back then, but also tony. I shopped at the Salvation Army Store fairly regularly. It was not that I needed to buy secondhand clothes, it was more likely another role. Looking back, I see that as much as I needed to be private I still wanted to be recognized. For now I was a dwarf, where once there had been a star.

***

One Saturday night after a meeting, a bunch of us decided to go to the Brown Derby. When the waiter came to take our drink orders, we all ordered coffee. Right away you could see his smile retract.

There were not servers then, just busboys and waiters. Obviously he thought his tip would be small. When he returned I caught his eye and he leaned close to me.

"You'll get a big tip, don't you worry."

"Thanks, Ma'am."

He looked at me a little closer.

"Hey, has anyone told you that you look exactly like Marilyn Monroe?

"Maybe a little older."

I smiled at him. "Thanks."

Just my luck there was a resurgence of interest in all things retro. Or maybe I never left the collective unconscious. I'm not sure. The "only a little older" piece of his dialogue initially startled me, an insane response I know, but which of us over 50 doesn't feel like we really look 35?

The moment's recognition meant more to me then I have ever admitted to myself. Though Reggie's nickname, Marilyn, had threatened my comfort for a good long while, now the feeling that there was still a little DNA left in there that resonated as the star, eased the constant anxiety over growing older that lived in my chest. I was afraid to be old, just not enough to kill myself as people always speculated.

A group of four at the table next to us looked my way and I found myself staring right into the eyes of Dean Martin -- though he, too, was quite a bit older. It was not true that he was drunk all the time, by the way. Just all the time he was not performing. Dean, Frank, Lawford -- memories boomeranged and bumped around in my head.

I looked away before Dean could focus on me. He had saved my ass on the last movie of my Twentieth Century contract and was another of my angels so far as I was concerned. I did not recognize the very young woman he was with. Two or three generations had come and gone in Hollywood by now. This girl was sleek with shaped biceps and triceps.

I excused myself and went to the Ladies Room. Two women were sharing a stall, snorting cocaine, I suspected. Nothing was the way it had been before. I was estranged from my home.

I returned to the table, mumbled something about a headache and went back to Chateau Marmont – but not before slipping the waiter a fifty-dollar bill. They still had not renovated the hotel and some of the French windows were kept closed by wires wound around the handles. I always thought they did that so people couldn't jump out of the windows. Later Belushi had no problem killing himself and I realized how ridiculous I was.

My Hollywood was gone. I was happy Marilyn was dead. I was beginning to know this new sober woman with no name, but her self-esteem was burgeoning. She was the best incarnation so far but not complete. I did not yet completely claim her.

OBJECT LESSON
Hollywood, February 17, 1982

Lee Strasberg's death deserves its own new page. Recall that even after I altered my will much money and costly items of mine were left to Lee with the instructions for him to distribute them, and to whom they would go.

After his death, it came to light quite publicly that Lee had warehoused everything I left, objet d'art, jewels, clothing, items that eventually brought in over three million dollars to Christie's. I will never know if any money actually made it to The Actor's Studio or if the Strasbergs used it as their own piggy bank.

My enmeshment with all the Strasbergs is its own story and has been written by Susan in a wonderful book titled *Marilyn and Me*. Her father began my discovery of the artiste that played Roslyn in *The Misfits*, an actor that would have gone on to play characters across the board and through all ages. But that actress was mine, not his and certainly not his wife, Paula's, though she tried to convince me that I could not succeed without her.

I don't speak ill of the dead. But Lee's betrayal of Marilyn's last wishes is symbolic of our entire relationship and of the attachments I made before I got well. For much of my life I was like the planet Venus, 900 degrees and emitting sulfuric acid

What people call high maintenance these days. (Just why did astronomers name this unapproachable star for the Goddess of love?) I was that way for many reasons but it all boiled down to a need for love. I needed you but I needed more for you to run away. This weakness left me available to a certain kind of predator, more crow than eagle.

Until Marilyn and the women I inhabited after her were laid to rest I was not equipped to connect to people of courage and integrity.

Days added up into all these years and I know now that alcohol quenched my courage and swept away my integrity, causing me to test everyone who tried to come near. Only those desperate enough to penetrate my toxins were around me in those years.

Symbiotic attachments were impossible and so I was a host for leeches and parasites. If I had been cogent, Lee would never have been the trustee of those assets.

The problem Lee kicked off haunted two generations. second wife, Anna, could not get her hands on those warehoused items. And so, in 1994 she sued for them but she lost and so nothing I owned was passed on to anyone I cherished, not my half-sister, Berniece, or Susan Strasberg or Pat Lawford. Nor did Susan's child, Jennifer Jones, receive a thing. What an enviable position I held, a dead person having the joy of seeing cherished objects passed on, but Lee's greed plus my need deprived all of us -- Object Lesson.

THE MISFIT
Venice, California, 1983-1985

West Hollywood where I rented a room is home to a special population and it was here I began to warm to Marilyn's importance to the gay community. It is her fragile sense of self, not her beauty that binds them to her. Back in the eighties when these people were not only disrespected but also dying they understood what it might be like to personify that sex is fun when you were dying inside, why you might want to kill the pain.

I felt at home with these people in the way I felt in my smoky rooms, though I had no way to show it.

Maybe this is why I signed on with a company that sent out Marilyn Monroe impersonators, often the gag entertainment at celebrations for a homosexual clientele. These patrons were not looking for gorgeous Marilyns. Rather they wanted Elvis in his fat days and Marilyn in drag.

I also got lots of calls for older men's parties, Korean War Vets who remembered Marilyn's visit to the war zone, where she performed in strapless dresses in the freezing cold. The arrival of me singing *Happy Birthday* and leaving a big red smooch on the celebrant's cheek could be a good break in the maudlin drinking.

I was amazed to learn that it was possible to live on a few hundred dollars a week. I lived precariously, no car, no health insurance, no dinners out, but I did get to the movies and I could go Dutch treat on a date so I was not obliged to sleep with anybody. Sounds absurd but that's the way things were in the '80s, never mind the so called Women's Movement.

In fact I sat out the Women's Movement. I don't think gals like Letty Pogrebin and Caroline Bird would have known what to do with me. Gloria Steinem was a different story. She and I had studied at the Actors' Studio together and I think that she was determined to be a performer — and she was — and is. Good for her. Not every actress needs a union card.

***

In May 1984, Gladys had a heart attack and died.

I heard about it first on public radio news when my radio alarm clock went off in the little room in West Hollywood. By this time Momma was out of the home in Florida and living with Berniece.

(God bless my darling half-sister who is going to flip her lid when she finds out I have been hiding out all these years!)

Berniece, forgive me. I want this book in your hands with a big lipstick kiss on it as soon as possible!

If you have lost a mother then you know how it feels. No matter how she treated you, a mother is the place where you incubate. I believe you can't hate your mother any more than the butterfly hates the confining chrysalis. We may kick and scream but in the end Mother is the name we cry out when we're in pain or terror.

A chronological look through Mother's pictures shows a typical smiling baby who very quickly develops the fathomless inward looking eyes of a person in anguish and painful introspection.

Look at Gladys's eyes. Drunks have these eyes, so that is how I know about them. If you are around recovering people long enough you will see how when they stay away from alcohol the eyes brighten up and you can begin to see the black pit fill up with light and promise.

Gladys wasn't a drinker, but she was bearing the burden of herculean psychic pain. There was no room for anything else, no love or motherhood, not sexual feeling, not creativity, only scraping the bottom of every single day on her knees moving toward I don't know what. Yet she lived long and into a graceful old age, a beautiful old lady.

I know Gladys loved me because for so long she had carried around a picture of Marilyn, showing it to other patients at Rockhaven and telling them I was her daughter.

Naturally the others thought she was cuckoo. This was the only way she had claimed me, but it was her way of loving. It had to be enough now. She was gone. I felt relief more than anything.

***

The royalties for all those images culled from *The Seven Year Itch* started accruing like mad. Look around any souvenir store anywhere. I get a little piece of each cup, lighter, hat, shirt, poster, magnet.

Back in the beginning of my life after Marilyn, even before Cherie Stoppard, I had rewritten the "found" will to shave off those royalties into the fund Joe held for me, overseen by his estate manager. It was eventually turned into an investment account in the name of Cherie Stoppard. I guess the lawyer thought Joe kept a mistress. It was into this account that the royalties flowed.

As the years went by, the percentages grew larger. I bought a yellow Arts and Crafts bungalow in Venice with its backyard on the canal near Mellenbacher Beach. This simple move into a one-bedroom 900 square-foot dwelling started my life over again. I got myself a dog from the CCPCA shelter, a blue-eyed part Australian Shepherd named, ironically, Joe. He was head shy, high-strung, and his nervous temperament brought out the calm in me. For the first time I was serene

. God bless that dog.

Joe and I carried on in that little cabin. I was ill equipped for much, but I had friends in church basements and somebody always needed a hand catering a party or babysitting. It was the happiest I had ever been. Inside I felt like the Marilyn Monroe pictured in Bert Fields' photos of me in sneakers and shorts before I became nothing but a symbol. Wide-eyed, open-hearted. That's who I was inside. Outside by now was another story. Do the arithmetic. I was 60 in 1986. I always knew it was time to color my hair when a glance in the mirror showed a graying, drooping woman with arthritic hands and feet and raccoon eyes,

But the bungalow took only just so much decorating and I had to fill my time. This was the only period of my life when I was totally single, no dates and no yearning. The animal shelter needed vet techs and I was a perfect candidate, as the primary requirement was not being afraid to clean up poop. So I went back to school to get certified.

Love saved me but it wasn't a man this time.

A doe-eyed mutt, part retriever and part something else, a midsized male, was dropped off in the middle of one March night, and left tied to the door.

I found him when I showed up at the pound in the morning to feed and muck out cages. He was submissive, and young, maybe 3 or 4.

He broke my heart just looking at him, needy and wanting only a scratched belly, a meal, not even thinking he could ever rate a home.

I took him into the shelter, cleaned him up, and when the vet came in the dog would not let go of me. All through the exam he didn't let up pushing his nose against my hand, insisting that I stay by his side. I felt love for him like a pain in my solar plexus. I couldn't let them take him into the general population to live in a cage. Whatever might have been this dog's history, he was saved now. I named him Homer and took him home to Joe, and the three of us made a family. I don't much care for cats but there was one mischievous female that I adopted to deal with the mice who felt entitled to stay on after I'd moved into the bungalow. She had been brought up with another cat, so I took them both.

My home was crowded but never lonely. I stayed in Venice longer than I had lived anywhere. I met my fate there.

ST. ALBANS MEMORIAL HOSPITAL
Portland, Oregon, 2011

Dr. Almador is examining my face.

He tells me much of my right cheek and upper lip will be replaced using the facial skin of a young boy just killed in a motorcycle accident, plus my own thigh skin and stem cells. The damaged nerves and muscles will also be replaced.

So in this circuitous way I have gotten my wish. The creature won't exist anymore. Not only will Marilyn Monroe disappear, but Norma Jean will acquire the face of a young boy.

My God has such a dry sense of humor.

I am not in such intense pain with the Fentanyl lollipops I take four times each day. I know that I will have to go through another detox because of them, and think I can't go through that again, can't we just call it a day? I'm 85. I don't have what it takes to get clean again. Honestly, I would rather die than go through detox again. But Almador tells me things are different now, there is a drug they will use to detox me.

So I will be saved from both deformity and death.

Is that a good thing? I'm not sure. I guess I'll find out when I can eat and kiss again. It is imperative that with healed lips I find someone to kiss.

And that I sing again.

I have not been kind to my body. While I was filming *How to Marry a Millionaire,* I was hit with appendicitis and I had the surgeon freeze my appendix to keep it stable for a few hours so I could continue the day's filming.

I had chloral hydrate enemas pumped into my rectum night after night to counteract the uppers I took all day.

Of course I drank barrels full of champagne from the time I became a party girl in Hollywood.

I added in the pills and never even thought there was anything odd about it. Just that the mix made it possible to turn off the pain and turn on the Start button in the morning.

Reboot, people call it now. Like I was any other machine.

So the idea of the operation is an abstraction. I'll be unconscious, then I'll wake up. I don't care about what happens in between. It's the coming to that terrorizes me. The months of healing and weaning off narcotics. The need to rebuild.

Cherie apparently has doubled some of her shifts. I have grown to love her. I will take her with me if I leave.

Of course I have no idea where I will go.

"Cherie, tell me a story."

"Madame, I am instructed for you to sleep. Sleep will heal you."

"You told your boys stories. Or did you sing lullabies?" Her eyes are dark brown, not black, like loam and fertile soil.

She laughs. "I did not tell my boys stories when they were young about my days spent in whorehouses."

I consider asking her to get me a fentanyl pain patch to add to the lollipop, even though it is not yet time. I can say I am having extra pain.

"You look like you are puzzling. You have a question?"

That's the trouble with good health care. The aides pay attention.

When writing in my journal doesn't silence the cravings, I get my cell phone out and start calling all the drunks I know in California. The ones who call me Cherie.

The first one I call is the woman who could never replace Sue, but who serves the same purpose in my life. She is responsible for my continued sobriety.

I'm 85 years old and a 50 year-old country and western singer is the woman I call when cravings and obsessions claim me. Paula is tall with blonde hair down to her waist and a husky voice.

She was born a boy in Texas.

She doesn't hold back about having her genitals removed. Once I had to ask her where she thought they put all those cast off male parts. We laughed until I peed in my pants and then she explained the whole business of accomplishing the change.

And here I am worrying about a little plastic surgery.

Paula has taught me that it is not only actors and fugitives who have to reshape their lives on the material plane.

And that it can be painful.

So bring on the new me, let's get it done, if the anesthesia doesn't befuddle me and the surgery doesn't kill me I'll just start over again.

CANDLE IN THE WIND
Venice, California, 1990-1999

It was getting tiresome, all of it. The starting over, the staying sober, the retrofitting my appearance and conversation and soul. I was surrounded by the veterinarians and other techs I worked with in the shelter and those people we called animal cops (The Environment Protection Agency). I was neighborly if not friendly with my neighbors. It's tough to share a canal with someone and not get to pass the time. Of course I was involved with other recovering drunks, but in the midst of all these people I was a still a stranger to myself. Despite our estranged relationship Mother's death had caused me to suffer a tearing away. I was 64. Too old to feel like an orphan yet there it was.

Around this time, I had what I would describe as a dalliance with a married man. Certainly not the first in my life. Consider all those stories about me. But this man was not glamorous or famous, he possessed none of the attributes that drew me to the flame. Elton John was wrong, actually, because in my Marilyn life I was not the candle so much as the thing mindlessly drawn to it. But now I had some idea of what I really wanted in a lover. The fact that he was someone else's mate made this a terrible choice, but I was at least sleeping with a man who liked me for who I was not what I could bring.

And for me, this was no dalliance since I gave as much as I could and I found places in myself where I had never traveled.

Here's what happened.

A few friends and I had started driving to a town outside of Las Vegas called Boulder City, built originally for the men building the Boulder dam. It is a small family town, no gambling allowed, maybe the only place near Vegas where there wasn't a slot machine in the ladies room. It is (or was) a sort of small Sedona or Woodstock, with stores selling crystals and a café that served only wine.

Of course, this is a long time ago and it is now somewhat of a destination. A young woman I mentor, just as Sue mentored me, Googled it and said it has tons of pages. I'm not sure how many 'tons' is, but I think it is a lot.

The café for me was the most important place.

My friends, Katherine L, Nancy D, and Martin O decided to take a trip to see the dam, we stopped at Boulder City for a meal at the town's family restaurant. The café had a sign in the window advertising for a singer for Saturday nights.

I saw someone inside the small space straightening up the round wrought iron tables. This was one of those times when something outside of myself maneuvered me into action. That first conversation with River Sabine is as fresh as the smell of Linden soap Cherie has just used to wash my hair.

I didn't even stop in a restroom to comb my hair. While my compadres waited outside, I knocked on the screen door and opened it, letting the October breeze push me in. The woman straightening up was about 6 feet tall. "I am interested in singing for the café," I said in a whispery voice not the same as the old me, but with the same impact. I was astonished but that's what came out. Just shows we really have not so much control over ourselves as we think.

She looked me over, took in my white sneakers, white cotton pants I bought from a Macy's catalogue. No doubt I was wearing a cotton knit sweater because I still had good boobs and made sure to buy effective bras though I of course didn't wear the sweaters as tight as before. And all of my clothes had sleeves, usually long or cap, because there is nothing worse than an older lady's upper arms, especially back then before what's-her-name made the Terminator movie with Governor Schwarzenegger and started the women's arms shape race. Few of us, including me, had done much work on the deltoids and triceps.

"Need to audition. Come back tomorrow at 7PM."

OK, so I had made the visual cut meaning they didn't need an ingénue.

"Great. Who do I ask for?"

"Ask for River, that's me. Bring music." Her head tilted towards a piano in the corner. My heart stopped. God help me, it was white. Had to be an omen.

If you don't know my white piano story, this won't mean anything but that's okay; it's not crucial and my fans will get it.

The group with me was all excited and we had planned to stay over anyway in a small inn, see the Dam, maybe creep into Las Vegas about 40 minutes away for an hour or so at the slot machines.

God I had hated Las Vegas,

I mean Marilyn had really hated that crowd. They were vulgar, let's face it, and no matter what she was promoting that brought her there, she felt ogled and harassed in a way different than in any other town.

I think people are drunk on everything in Las Vegas, not only booze and drugs, but sex, gambling, the absence of clocks — the nighttime of people comes out there.

But the group wanted to play the slots, so I stayed in the inn and thought about what to sing.

Though there was never any doubt about what I would sing, I didn't have music. I opted to sing without accompaniment.

So long, it had been so long since I had sung anything. I did not even let myself sing in the shower or to the radio. First it was too painful, then the music was too strange, then Reggie was the musician.

I don't know what kept me from singing after that, except maybe that the singer had hidden right along with Marilyn.

I was rusty but doubted Boulder City had heard *Diamonds Are A Girl's Best Friend* sung quite so much as Marilyn Monroe could sing it. So Saturday nights found me in Boulder City's Café for a few years after that.

My lifelong phobia about performing had not lifted, but it was easier to face.

Having aged, lost husbands and lovers, left my career, my identity, it was a cinch to live through stage fright. If only we could look young and be old at the same time which I guess is what plastic surgery is all about, and now that I think of it exactly what I'll be doing with that young man's face.

But I was writing about the married man.

The man who captured my heart was an Indian. He taught and coached basketball on a reservation in the vicinity of Boulder City. Gary was tall, dark and handsome. A hero.

He was kind and a good person. He had beautiful manners. He was smart and had a great sense of humor.

The only problem is that he had an Indian wife and two young children. We would get together on the nights I was not singing and he was not coaching, eat dinner far away from Boulder City or the Reservation, because he was afraid of being seen with me. This hurt my feelings. But I was enraptured. Sex was different with Gary. Not with Reggie or any one of the short term lovers since him had I been so pleasured.

Along with sex my curves made a comeback or maybe it was my walk. I always had great muscles from working with the animals. Imagine Marilyn Monroe as your grandmother with softer lines, the same look in her eyes, an up-do, jeans and running shoes. Vintage sweaters.

My love affair with Gary restored my glow. I felt centered, my head in the clouds but my feet on the ground.

An odd sequence of events concurred that reaffirms my belief that nothing happens by accident. Once I started at the café we were packed for two or three years each Saturday night until a new place opened in town with games and live, loud music. Most likely it was punk or trash or garage, maybe heavy metal, I am not acquainted with the difference. They stole our show. It was only a question of time before River had to close up shop.

One night right before closing a man came shuffling in who kept his head down, but sat very close to the piano. He reeked so of alcohol that I could smell him. My heart broke for him. He made a request for an old song that Reggie used to sing. I was rusty on the words but the pianist was younger than I and picked up the slack. When he faltered, the stranger pitched in. I never gave it a second thought.

The next day Gary met me in Boulder City to say he could not go on with our affair, it was killing his conscience and would I please understand.

There's a prayer we like in the healing rooms that teaches us to love, understand and forgive rather than to seek those comforts from someone else. I don't pray as often as I should but I prayed that night for Gary and I prayed for his wife and the next day I felt better, even a little relieved. This made me feel like maybe I wasn't such a bad person after all. I was ready to have no job and no lover, just my animals and bungalow. But life had other plans.

***

Joe died of lung cancer in August of '99.

No one informed me because only his son knew of my existence and Joey was still living an addict's life. In coverage of the funeral I saw that Joey was one of the pall bearers.

Perhaps they had reconciled at the end.

I regretted that I had not been able to help Joey, but there was much outreach where he was and the information had come back to me via semaphore about DiMaggio's son living in SRO's and resisting help, going straight back on the street any time he was detoxed.

He wasn't ready.

I suffered great remorse over the death of Joe DiMaggio, mourning what we never were able to be to each other except on the world's stage.

Joe was lost after his baseball career was over and he spent forever looking for himself.

When he died, I cried for all of us because the hero had slipped away years before and we hadn't even noticed it.

***

Six months later Joey followed his father into the hereafter.

I got news through the reliable network that keeps drunks apprised of each other's wellbeing. Joey had died of a heart attack. He was 57 years old. I looked the obituary up on the internet, an instrument of torture so far as I'm concerned but it serves some purpose. No details were given other than he had "struggled with substance abuse and gone through periods of homelessness." This served for me as a wakeup call.

Nothing is complete, just the universe. We are all prey to the daily possibilities of tragedy and trauma. That's life, not movies. Part of me had recovered from the black magic of Hollywood when I disappeared, but there were lingering side effects, one of them being a refusal to accept the hand life dealt me. I had shaped a certain identity in the years following my disappearance, but I still had not dug down any deeper than recovering from being Marilyn. Now I was forced to look at the woman who remained after I stripped away Norma Jean, Marilyn, Cherie Stoppard, and whoever it was who was living in Venice and hanging out in an animal shelter.

Everyone knows the struggle I had with endometriosis, miscarriages, and an ectopic pregnancy. Nowadays I suspect I would have had fertility treatments and made some poor child miserable and crazy; some things are better left undone. I was not mother material. But as I said to begin with, Joey was like my nephew. By now I was way past grateful that he had saved my life.

Why hadn't I tried to help him? If I had wanted to nurture Joey, why had he ended up dead in the street? Questions like these returned, changed to demons and self-loathing.

I cursed myself, went underground, and even the animals couldn't reach me. Alcohol called my name.

For days I stayed in the loft bed of the bungalow where the yellow California light moved across me predictably. My mind was hydra-fractured and toxic thoughts spilled out. Paula and others left long messages, but I lacked the wherewithal to use the telephone. I was suspended in a different realm. The urge to self-medicate was fierce, but I held on.

The problem was, I initially saw Joey's death as a lost opportunity *for me.* Ultimately I realized that I was thinking only of myself, and I snapped out of it. I recognized this as a slip in my own empowerment, a return to Marilyn's narcissism and self-centered grieving. I was able to see how far I had come and how much life there might be left to carry me further.

It's a shame, in a way, that I had to disappear when I was so crazy and young. I ultimately reached an essential part hidden until my 70s. I was a new person entirely, and yet I had to keep the juicy part away from the world.

So I moved on.

But not alone.

CONSEQUENCES
Venice/Beverly Hill, 2000-2011

The fire was definitely set on purpose.

As it fed on itself -- and the straw in the cages and hay in the stalls -- we were trying to free the dogs and cats.

The firemen were hosing down the dog section of the building and one of them was shooing us out, opening cages beside us. The animals were scratching and clawing to get free and I just let them bite and claw.

The Rottweilers and pit-bulls reverted to their nature. These were animals in danger and so they became dangerous. I would not leave the shelter until the last cage was opened. Still, we lost half of the animals, some from smoke in their lungs and others that burned to death in the cages.

Each one took away a piece of me. In fact, the last dog I freed, a pure bred German Shepherd, lunged at me rather than rushing for the exit.

It would be impossible to list all the animals that claimed a part of me that day. They are all gone now, perished in the fire that also trashed my face.

***

At the turn of the century I was 74, an awkward stage, too old to be a Cougar and too young for the body I was in.

I began to study young women, their smooth necks, graceful hands uncrippled by arthritis, and finally I got the cosmic joke—we don't know anything important until we are too dried up and post menopausal to use it.

That's about the time I fell in love again, remarried, and became a grandma.

I had married Dougherty at sixteen to keep from having to go back to an orphanage. I had married DiMaggio because there was a scandal brewing about me and I wanted to look good to the censors. Miller was an aberration.

Love came this time when I didn't care about it. When I looked in the mirror, I could never be sure if I would see the young face or the old one. It depended on the mirror, the light, the amount of sugar I had eaten the day before. My mood was constant, stable. I would have loved a good drama to come along, but those days were over. I had forgotten about the passion, the rush of warmth, peace and simultaneous insanity that could accompany a touch from a loved one. Just a touch would be enough, I was thinking. Then I met Jules.

Jules Lawrence. An LA Criminal Attorney who had sold his practice when he turned seventy in order to spend his years as a grandpa with his wife of forty years only to watch her die from a massive heart attack three months later. I remember that Sue always said to me if you hold on to the wheel of life it keeps turning and eventually the good times return. And the bad ones.

I thought of this immediately when Jules and I met at a friend's barbecue. He seemed low key, but I was to learn that beneath the surface was a man who loved and raged with the same intensity.

There was nothing quiet about Jules except his presentation. We bumped into each other at the open bar, where both of us were ordering seltzer with lime.

I was still missing a screw in my head from grieving for all those in my life who had so recently died. I was aware there were wounds in the fabric of my spirit that needed sewing up. Jules was undone some other place not so obvious from the outset.

He still smoked. I found that horrifying. Nevertheless, we talked over seltzer and his cigarettes for a good few hours that day. Looking back I suspect that Barbara and her partner Stefanie, who eventually became her wife, had planned the rendezvous and just had not bothered to tell us.

At first he visited me, traveling from his palace in Beverly Hills to my menagerie in Venice.

Jules loved my creatures.

I loved his mind.

My intellect had remained fierce since my years in college. Now, with no fear of discovery and royalties from the tchotchkes for just that one movie piling up, plus gains from the investments made on behalf of the "Cherie Stoppard" account, my brain had room to roam.

The lust astonished me. It might be embarrassing to read but not with any one since Reggie had this old lady been naked in bed so many hours of the day. After all, Gary was a married man. My female parts were still working. I was in love with Jules' privates. I don't know how this happened to me.

My appearance changed once again.

Marilyn Monroe, a grandmother with softer lines, her hair gone natural grey, the same look in her eyes as all people in recovery have, direct and in your face. I started wearing lipstick and stopped using the foundation I had worn for a few years. My complexion glowed. I wore my hair so it looked like I had that widow's peak in front, the way it did in the early years, and in layers of waves past my neck. I was still in jeans but now past the running shoes phase, I was into Eccos and God help me, I owned a pair of Birkenstocks (no socks).

I was a sex goddess for real now.

I hear that as people get older they live more in the past, but I had spent many years chewing that over with shrinks seven days a week until I went mad.

This old lady was looking forward.

So Jules and I made a plan.

This is the part of the journal that I have to get down before they take me into surgery in case something unfortunate happens.

I had another fellow traveler who had been following me for some time.

We came face to face while I was with the dogs on the boardwalk seated for a moment to catch my breath. Nothing is like the Venice boardwalk. No longer an actress, I had become a storyteller. I would make up stories about the lives of the people walking by and then hear their dialogue in my head. I was long since over the fear that I was a schizophrenic, and giving different voices to all these characters amused me.

So I was alone on the boardwalk when the beaten down old man with disheveled white hair and a drunkard's nose came into focus. I recognized him first as the man from the café who had come in late to request a song. There was no avoiding his stare so I smiled and then I knew.

Cassy, an Australian Shepherd I had adopted a year before, cowered beneath the bench making a scary sound that seemed to emanate from her diaphragm like the *chi* of a martial artist.

Reggie, for now I was sure it was he, slowly limped toward me and sat down. I could smell the alcohol though I had the impression that he was not yet drunk. Cassy was more aggressive, and growled low in her throat until I gave her a command to stay down.

"You left me for dead" was how the conversation started.

And who could blame him?

I suggested we go for a walk so I could smell out whether he was dangerous or see if he wanted something. But he gestured to his leg and explained he had trouble with his legs because he was diabetic.

I was calculating how much it would cost to get rid of him but he had either read my mind or gone through this with someone else, because he put his hand on my forearm and shook his head.

"No. Don't be scared. I don't want anything, just talk."

He explained a bit about how he had married and had a kid but had never been able to stay sober. But the Rome thing, that was so strange. He had been in a coma, and after two days of being considered a lost cause, he'd opened his eyes and asked for me.

"No," they'd repeatedly told him in response to the question he'd posed again and again.

"Nobody's been here to see you."

My stomach flew into my heart or the other way around from the guilt. And shame.

I had no excuse other than I was a different woman back then, thinking only of myself and how I needed to escape, but Reggie knew nothing about my history.

So all I could say was, "I was newly sober. What can I do to make it up to you?"

But he merely shrugged.

Eventually I convinced him to have a cup of coffee and realized he was not homeless or without funds, so that was a relief. I did not ask any personal questions. We bought coffee from a stand and talked about inconsequentials.

He called me Marilyn. That made me want to run which was ridiculous, of course. Reggie did not know who I was, this was only his nickname for me. I said the dogs needed feeding and nearly ran back home. That night in the meeting room I raised my hand and talked about regretting the past.

I saw no need to bring this up with Jules. We had been together long enough to fall in love but what we had was on the fragile side of forever. I had never made it to the other side with any one, you know, for better or worse, in sickness and health, til death, and I did not want to rock the boat.

So, Jules.

Here was the plan.

Beverly Hills by the week and Venice on weekends.

Dogs plus his cat.

But here was the clincher. His son Kilby, and daughter-in-law lived in San Diego, where Kilby made documentary films as funding tools for nonprofit agencies.

His grandchild had been born just the past April, Josephine.

"Her hair is red."

That was the first thing he told me about her, right at that party, flipping through the photos on his iPhone.

"'I hate these contraptions."

He was stumbling over the touch-free component,

but I saw enough photos to know that there was a little munchkin around, and that was why I said yes when he asked if we could get together for dinner in Venice the day after the barbecue.

I don't know what it's like to feel your DNA replicated and to hold that replication in your arms.

Or to be separated from that creature.

I only know that Josephine taught me more than I had learned from just about anybody else. She would not hold my hand unless it was her pleasure. I was not good at changing her diaper so she fussed if it was my turn.

When she was a year old I stopped being nervous about pushing her in the swing. We put up the most intricate playset we could find in Jules's backyard and Josie managed to reengineer it, I guess is the word, using only the slide, swings and drums, ignoring more complex and rather stupid accoutrements.

Josephine was real, something I had taken 75 years to become.

Every weekend was split between Venice and San Diego, but Josephine was always there.

The dogs worried me because she was crawling by then and either one could push her over, but nothing scared the baby and in no time everybody was acclimated. I left my job at the shelter, which had always been more something they did for me than the opposite. Often, though, I just stopped by to catch up on everyone. This never changed.

Occasionally, I would also check up on the humans who worked there.

Jules and I decided to get married one weekend while watching Josie seated on her blanket next to a beagle mix I had brought home to foster for the weekend.

There was a small gift-wrapped surprise waiting for me when I joined Jules in the loft we used, to stay clear of the bedroom when Josephine was napping.

There was that Harry Winston box again. I had never had a formal engagement and I'd never had a man get on his knees and propose to me. With a canal gurgling in the background, no less. I cried real tears. I reached down and smoothed the piece or two of his grey hair and realized he was crying too.

I think Jules was certain when his wife died he would never find anyone to love again and in his mind I had appeared like an angel. And of course he was the prince plus the knight I had been searching for all my life. I thought to myself if I die right now my life will be complete. But that wasn't what was in store for me.

***

I am being weaned off the dope and feeling really crappy and crabby. I don't know how normal people feel, but detoxing is hell for recovering addicts, who can't metabolize narcotics normally.

My head is not yet clear and my bloodstream is screaming out for a shutdown switch.

The anxiety stabs whatever part of my spirit is located in my stomach.

The sensation is as psychological as it is physical and I am sure that an abundance of adrenalin has flooded my brain.

I need to keep moving my legs, and occasionally I feel panicked and want to jump out of bed and run, so drastic is my need for flight.

This is the detox hell that Joey fled from. The hell that Sue escaped with over 30 years of abstinence. If I were not locked up here in the hospital, I would not be able to stay away from something to ease the pain.

I think of Reggie's need to take action against me to ease his anxiety and tumultuous feelings and I begin to forgive and understand.

***

The Girl amazingly reappeared in my life with Jules. I dyed my hair again.

I was about as glamorous an old lady one could be in southern California outside of Hollywood, which isn't saying much, but I returned or re-found or rediscovered the femme fatale and now she was mine.

We were rich, and I shopped on Rodeo Drive like all the other Hollywood dolls. I stuck to off-the-rack couture with pronounceable names — Givenchy, Dior, once in a while Versace, though Donatella never could replace her brother in my opinion, poor man. Generally when not in jeans I wore dress slacks in neutral colors and kitten heels while everyone else wore extremely expensive open shoes or sandals.

The reason for the shoes was that one awful degeneration about me was that over the years my feet had crippled up with arthritis and developed huge bunions.

The first time I dared to unveil my naked feet to Jules in the light was way after we had been intimate. He thought my insistence on lovemaking in the dark, no matter where it took place, was due to my aged body. But no, it was the battered feet, abused by those years in stilettos.

Or maybe they somaticized my fugitive status. Nor had my hands been spared.

To some degree, I was like any old crone.

But well dressed and pampered with facials, good haircuts, and that huge diamond ring.

The feet actually were the gateway to my telling Jules that I had been Marilyn Monroe. We were at that common early stage of love affairs where people reveal their darkest secrets.

He had cross-dressed a few times not because he had questions about his sexuality but because the lingerie compelled him. I found this hilarious.

Many women won't remember girdles, which were really tummy bands without the help of surgical intervention -- industrial strength spandex. I never wore them, and that was part of Marilyn's appeal. She was allowed to swish, and because I wore no panties, the fabric of my clothes was right up against my skin. I could not keep a straight face at the thought of Jules trying on the corset he described as coming from, naturally, Frederick's of Hollywood.

I believe he tried on his mother's proper lady's pumps and a long-line brassiere. He had been sixteen. No online pornography then, no naked girls on TV. I don't know what ground he was testing, but it was another reminder that we all at some point wear a costume.

The ugly feet, he said, could not compare to this twisted secret cave.

A force outside of myself spoke through me and said, "I am not Cherie Stoppard.

" I am Marilyn Monroe."

Who said that? I was thinking, but the relief of more than a lifetime fell away. I had been Marilyn from 1946 to 1962.

It was 2000, more than six times as long as I had been her I had been others.

Crystalizing.

If I had been a butterfly, my caterpillar would have started in the prehistoric age.

I relive this now, remembering his beautiful aged face sketched with the lines of an enormous life well lived. Once the words were out it occurred to me that the revelation might bring horrible consequences.

There's that word—my whole life was spent learning there are consequences, having Ed Digby fall in love with me way back when had caused him pain. Leaving Reggie for dead in Rome triggered the craziness that set the fire that landed me here in Portland.

What consequences might this truth bring?

Naturally the truth of consequences (hah!) was trust. Jules didn't doubt my story or rush me to a psychiatrist. Best of all, it brought us closer. It seemed like from then on whatever we said to each other was taken at face value, as though we had never learned to be human and lie, sneak, manipulate, hurt, despise.

So with my secret revealed, he went to the kitchen of the Beverly Hills house and got himself a beer and me a big bottle of sparkling water, and I told him my whole story.

It took hours.

By the time we finished two rounds of drinks he knew everything and I had to pee.

That was that.

End of story.

For our honeymoon we went to Hawaii. We stayed in a small hotel on a beach in Kauai that no one used. I could never figure out why. Each morning a wild rooster woke us up and we took our rented jeep down to a surfers' beach.

It was so exhilarating that I was famished after watching them. We found a breakfast place. Our waitress had given her life over to surfing. It was the centripetal force of her days.

To me, she looked like the archetype.

Always in neat cutoffs and tee shirts, her body was that copper color that is fantastic until you reach middle age and then it's just wrinkled and cancerous.

I thought she was bright, and after I worked through my intolerance I discovered I felt for someone giving up their life for a stupid sport, I realized that I too had given my life over to a fantasy.

And I had lived it out.

The sun was much too strong for us non-Hawaiians so Jules and I mostly stayed indoors at a splashy hotel near ours where tropical fish swam around the hotel restaurant in a tubular aquarium, a cornucopia, a medley.

All the pools at this five star hotel were beyond infinity. They were ludicrous, really, with slides and waterfalls.

All I wanted to do was swim and eat.

We stayed in Kauai, and on the plane home we vowed that we would next go to Alaska in June, when the sun never set.

Jules was lured back to work for a year to defend a colleague indicted for murdering his commitment partner in an argument over what was served for dinner. The evidence was circumstantial, but the prosecutor had a reputation for winning even those cases others considered unwinnable.

As it happened, I knew the murdered man from the rooms. He had told us that he had reason to believe his commitment partner had another lover, also one of the tribe who had started using heroin again.

It was much more probable that this lover was the guilty one. For me, that presented a huge dilemma. Anonymity is the basic principle that had successfully protected me for 34 years. Was I then to break someone else's anonymity? And to repeat something told in confidence?

Obviously the client was not telling Jules that his deceased partner had been in the healing rooms. I spoke to Sue, Paula, and other people who knew the principles involved. Talking to Jules about any of this didn't feel right until I had processed the, alright, *consequences* of the decision.

Anyway he was so busy working that he was never around to talk to. This was irony. After all was said and done, I was a person with ordinary problems: my marriage was coming apart, I could not eat or sleep. For months, Jules and I did not eat a meal together, or read the Sunday paper, snuggling next to each other on the couch.

Josephine would never have seen him if I hadn't picked her up and brought her to him, wherever he was at the time. And even then he was absent. I began to wonder if I had made a horrible mistake.

But then it hit me—I *was* making the mistake. I was holding out on him. He was struggling and I had the answer.

I writhed and twisted a few days more, and then appeared at his office downtown, making sure I dressed not like a wife but a witness. I wore a navy suit with a pencil skirt, a tight, short jacket, and a pair of Lanvin flats. Eighty still looked good, if I do say so myself. I waited to be announced like any other client and then told him what I knew.

Case closed. Lover had no alibi and his DNA was found everywhere. No Anonymity broken. My *husband* was home and that word began to take on a new meaning. Truly Jules was my only husband ever, my mate and partner. It took me eighty years but what the hell. I finally got it right.

***

By 2000, it seemed like everyone had died. Now the DiMaggios were gone, Then early in the year Sue was gone. And laid to rest, too, was my worst nightmare: the child who clung to an insane mother, who married a man to stay out of an orphanage, and then survived only because other people told her who she was and how to be. She was gone, and in her place was a sober woman with no fears she couldn't face and no place she couldn't travel to that didn't have people offering safety and acceptance in the healing rooms.

FIRE

Jules died like a grandfather should.

We kept a little boat on the bank of the canal so Josie and Jules could go exploring. Josie was ten. I was 83. Not long ago I saw a rendering of myself as I would look at 80 and it was pretty close. Still blonde, wrinkles following the contours of the glorious smile that hid all the pain. Beauty mark removed since it was no longer fashionable and in any event, at some point a dermatologist had suggested it should be removed. The rendering showed my eyes a bit droopy at the upper lids and outer edges, but still with a timeless something or other. Of course the artist neglected the obvious — that I would have had my entire being redone by surgeons, but I'd been saved from that. Until now. I liked my old woman face.

There have always been dogs and now there were two rescued retrievers, Katrina dogs that were puppies the day Jules died. I was schooling them, or more likely picking up poop, so when Jules, Kilby and Josephine came in for a drink after a dip in the canal, I didn't notice that his face was the wrong color, pale with fierce splotches of blood like war paint on each cheek.

He died right there, sinking to the kitchen floor with all of us around him. Kilby knew CPR but Jules was dead before he hit the floor. . There we were, me calling 911 on my cell phone, weeping -- no acting there -- and the puppies thinking he was playing, slobbering all over his hands and face.

Josephine was the most together person there, what with her grandfather dead and me hovering over him, trying to hold onto him, not ready to accept that he had gone so fast without even saying goodbye.

Yet nothing came undone.

People came from all over -- family, friends, Jules' colleagues. I had played this moment out countless times over the years we were together, written it many different ways, and always I was helpless, looking to others to act on my behalf, though it never occurred to me to wonder who.

I was treated like the principal here even though Jules had center stage. And though it might seem callous to think of it that way, it helped me get through the ritual. Soon enough, I was a functioning widow, panicked much of the time and desolate the rest.

But I was still standing and less dead then I had been August 5, 1962.

***

It was obvious from the minute the investigation began that the fire was set.

This is the first time I have announced who I believe did it, and that is only because I have learned he also perished soon after. I have struggled with announcing it even as I wrote this, but no one can hurt him anymore.

Ask anyone who has struggled with alcohol or drug addiction. Reggie's life was one long torment. He did not need more punishment.

Here's what happened. A few months after Jules's death I was stopping at the shelter for a visit, and just this once, thank God, Josephine was not with me.

Or perhaps, now that I think of it, Reggie took the opportunity of the child not being there to act.

That is far more likely.

After Jules died, she still came to visit me. Had she shared my DNA, I couldn't have loved her more, and I consider myself undeservedly fortunate – okay, blessed -- that she would say the same thing.

I saw Reggie every so often on the boardwalk. We would have coffee and I would try to talk him into going to a meeting with me. It never occurred to me that he had the wherewithal to follow me, a broken down old Volvo, illegally on the road I am sure, that someone had given him.

I never saw smoke or flames until I was inside the kennel beyond the waiting and medical areas. It was my habit to go back and see which animals had been adopted since the last time and introduce myself to the new ones. There was a terrier, unremarkably named Terry, honestly, not my favorite breed, but she had the brightest black eyes and funny white eyebrows, who had been dropped off the week before.

I was squatting all the way down, crippled knees having a good day, when the dogs, in unison, began barking. Then there were flames. Later on as I lay in the burn unit at good old Cedars Sinai I remembered I saw a man walk in to the kennel very briefly. I would have sworn he was wearing a black watch cap, but that must have been my fervent imagination seizing on the old OJ Simpson trial.

Should I have known he was that dangerous? I might have known he had not forgiven me for leaving him for dead, and in his shoes I'm sure I would have felt the same. But it was the animals frying, baking, and screaming in the fire and smoke that made me consider turning him in. After I regained consciousness I mulled over what to do. I didn't care so much about my face. I had outlived vanity. It was those helpless creatures' torment that made me want him to go through hell. But I've been there and I knew he already was going through it.

I don't know how long I've been out of surgery, but when I come to I am immediately conscious. It took maybe three days to get back to this journal. The end is coming. The pain is awesome. I am either going to look like this beautiful young man plus me or I am going to die from whatever old people die of in hospitals.

Or I will hate the way I look and then I guess I'll just live with it. I wanted to kill myself for so long, and then I died and got over it. I wanted the creature killed and it took some doing, but she left as I lived from the inside out.

Jules would have loved to see this metamorphosis. He was a pragmatist and the science of a face transplant would have been much more interesting than whether I looked like Frankenstein or Marilyn Lawrence. Or Cherie Stoppard. Marilyn Monroe Stoppard Lawrence. The name change started in Ben Lyon's office at Twentieth Century Fox in 1946 when he decided I should pick the name Mary Lynn, and it's been changing ever since. No one alive would call me Marilyn Monroe anymore. But she still exists.

Look at all the people who still love her.

***

ABOUT THE AUTHOR

The Memoir of Marilyn Monroe is Sandi Gelles-Cole's latest foray into fiction, building on her more than 35 years' as a book editor, ghostwriter, and book doctor. She began her publishing career in 1973 with the David McKay Company and later held editorial positions with Dutton/NAL, Rawson Associates, and Dell. In 1983, she founded her editorial agency, Gelles-Cole Literary Enterprises, which continues to provide editorial services to agents, publishers, and authors. Over the course of her career, she has edited more than 500 novels and nonfiction books, including more than a dozen bestsellers, an Edgar Award nominee, and a BlackBoard Book of the Year award-winner, among others. The Memoir of Marilyn Monroe is her second novel.